SPOOKIEST STORIES EVER

SPOOKIEST STORIES EVER

FOUR SEASONS OF KENTUCKY GHOSTS

ROBERTA SIMPSON BROWN
AND LONNIE E. BROWN

FOREWORD BY ELIZABETH TUCKER

THE UNIVERSITY PRESS OF KENTUCKY

Scholarly publisher for the Commonwealth,
serving Bellarmine University, Berea College, Centre
College of Kentucky, Eastern Kentucky University,
The Filson Historical Society, Georgetown College,
Kentucky Historical Society, Kentucky State University,
Morehead State University, Murray State University,
Northern Kentucky University, Transylvania University,
University of Kentucky, University of Louisville,
and Western Kentucky University.
All rights reserved.

Editorial and Sales Offices: The University Press of Kentucky
663 South Limestone Street, Lexington, Kentucky 40508-4008
www.kentuckypress.com

14 13 12 11 10   5 4 3 2 1

Library of Congress Cataloging-in-Publication Data

Brown, Roberta Simpson, 1939–
    Spookiest stories ever : four seasons of Kentucky ghosts / Roberta
Simpson Brown and Lonnie E. Brown, foreword by Elizabeth Tucker.
       p.   cm.
    ISBN 978-0-8131-2595-4 (hardcover : alk. paper)
    1. Tales—Kentucky. 2. Ghost stories, American—Kentucky. I. Brown,
Lonnie E. II. Tucker, Elizabeth, 1948– III. Title.
  GR110.K4B76 2010
  398.209769—dc22
                                2010017533

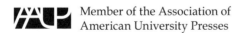 Member of the Association of
American University Presses

To all our family and friends, living and dead,
who shared their stories with us;
to the readers who will pass them on;
and in memory of our friends,
Karen Harrigan and Drewry Meece Jr.

CONTENTS

FOREWORD

In *Spookiest Stories Ever,* Roberta Simpson Brown and Lonnie
E. Brown invite us to join their circle of family members and
friends for some spine-tingling storytelling. The organiza-
tion of their stories reminds us how important it is to stay
in touch with the changing seasons—even nowadays, when
television, central heating, air conditioning, and electric
lights are apt to make us less aware of what is happening
outdoors. This wonderful collection of ghost stories brings
us back to an earlier era, when storytelling provided one of
the main forms of entertainment. During sultry summer
evenings, relatives would gather in their backyard to enjoy
cool breezes and swap stories. When fall winds blew cold
and leaves covered the ground, chairs around the warm fire-
side replaced lawn chairs. Winter holidays gave families time
to tell their favorite ghost tales. In the spring, as the natural
world bloomed, storytelling moved outside once more.

Those of us who love ghost stories find them both intriguing and significant. Through them, a dimension of won-

der enters our lives. As folklorist Barbara Walker explains in her book *Out of the Ordinary*, "we live in an imprecise and ambiguous world, which in its inexactitude allows for the awesome, the inexplicable, the wondrous" (xi). It is exciting to recall moments when extraordinary events have suggested the presence of the supernatural. Within family circles and groups of friends, people tell stories about amazing encounters with ghosts. Through the efforts of students and scholars, many of these stories have found a permanent home in folklore archives.

Folklorists' publication of stories from these archives has familiarized readers with the distinctive character of Southern ghost stories. W. K. McNeil's *Ghost Stories from the American South* (1985) offers a representative selection, including stories of ghosts from the Revolutionary War and the Civil War. In his introduction, McNeil explains that, first, spirits of the dead "may come back in the same body they had while alive; second, they may appear in some sort of spectral form; third, they may be invisible and known only by the deeds, noises or mischief they commit" (3). Because ghost stories function as cultural artifacts, they give us important information about Southern culture, which combines Anglo-American, African-American, and Hispanic-American elements as well as traditions of other ethnic groups (23).

Since the publication of William Lynwood Montell's *Ghosts along the Cumberland: Deathlore in the Kentucky Foothills* (1975), American readers have known that Kentucky provides a favorable setting for ghost stories. Montell's book presents folklore of the supernatural from Kentucky's eastern "Penny-royal" district, near the Tennessee border. In his introduction, Montell notes the transition from rural to urban life that took place after World War II. "Despite the fascination of a new way of life," he explains, "these people of the soil have managed to cling tenaciously to many of the older forms of folk traditions" (ix). Among these valued traditions are omens of imminent death, customs associated with the time and manner of death, rituals for preparation of the corpse, and guidelines for funerals and burial.

Montell has also published other substantial collections of Kentucky ghost stories. *Ghosts across Kentucky* (2000) includes tales of headless ghosts, animal ghosts, murder and suicide victims, and vanishing hitchhikers, among other supernatural entities. He devotes one chapter to Civil War ghosts and another to ghosts of colleges and universities. His *Haunted Houses and Family Ghosts of Kentucky* (2001) presents fascinating accounts of ghosts in homes large and small across the state. Told as renditions of true experience, these stories give readers a clear sense of Kentuckians' interest in the supernatural.

Another author who has made Kentucky ghost stories better known is Alan Brown, whose book *Haunted Kentucky: Ghosts and Strange Phenomena of the Bluegrass State* was published in 2009. One of his earlier books, *Shadows and Cypress: Southern Ghost Stories* (2000), presents detailed, exciting ghost stories that reflect Southern culture and history. His *Ghost Hunters of the South* (2006) introduces the reader to forty-four ghost-hunting groups that have generated interesting stories.

An important difference between the present volume and the books just mentioned is that the Browns tell stories from their own family and friends. Many of the stories here reflect the storytellers' relationships to people who have passed away. "My First Ghost," for example, is the story of a child's journey home from school through a severe thunderstorm. Jim, an elderly friend, guides the frightened child from a dangerous location under a tree to a safe spot in a gully. Later, the child learns that Jim died before the storm. This story, and others here, offer consolation, suggesting that love can transcend the boundary of death.

Other stories in the Browns' book remind us of the need for justice. In "The Floating Shawl," for example, a mother and her baby mysteriously disappear. Were they murdered, or did they simply go away? When the authors' Uncle Buck sees a shawl floating by, he wonders whether the spirits of the mother and child have come to tell him that they had been killed. As in other stories, the mystery remains unsolved.

Through the talented, kind-hearted narrators of these stories, readers of this book become part of Kentucky's storytelling community and participate in this state's rich traditional heritage. Readers are sure to find this book both meaningful and enjoyable.

Elizabeth Tucker
Department of English, Binghamton University

Works Cited

Brown, Alan. *Ghost Hunters of the South.* Jackson: University Press of Mississippi, 2006.

——. *Haunted Kentucky: Ghosts and Strange Phenomena of the Bluegrass State.* Mechanicsburg, Pa.: Stackpole Books, 2009.

——. *Shadows and Cypress: Southern Ghost Stories.* Jackson: University Press of Mississippi, 2000.

McNeil, W. K. *Ghost Stories from the American South.* New York: Dell, 1985.

Montell, William Lynwood. *Ghosts across Kentucky.* Lexington: University Press of Kentucky, 2000.

——. *Ghosts along the Cumberland: Deathlore in the Kentucky Foothills.* Knoxville: University of Tennessee Press, 1975.

——. *Haunted Houses and Family Ghosts of Kentucky.* Lexington: University Press of Kentucky, 2001.

Walker, Barbara. *Out of the Ordinary: Folklore and the Supernatural.* Logan: Utah State University Press, 1995.

ACKNOWLEDGMENTS

Many individuals besides the authors contribute to the making of any book, and we are grateful to all who helped us. We especially thank our friends, Robert W. Parker, Racheal Ogan, Sharon Brown, Jackie Atchison, and Thomas Freese, who are always ready to help us search for tales to tell. We thank the storytellers who have died but live on in the stories they shared with us. We appreciate the support we have received from the University Press of Kentucky, especially Laura Sutton, who was there helping us every step of the way, and Donna Bouvier, who did an outstanding job editing this book.

Many others helped us with kindness, inspiration, and support while we were in the process of creating this book. Our thanks to both friends (especially Jerry Anderson, Mary Ann Ballard, Cathy Bohler, Marian Call, Grover and Linda Gaddie, Lori Graham of Alley Cat Café and Catering, Deanna Hansen, Anne Howard, Donna Ising, Denise Kirzinger, Norma Lewis, Shirley Meece, Robin Miller, Lynwood

Acknowledgments

Montell, Lee and Joy Pennington, Joan Todd, and Candy and Dennis Wilson) and family (especially Charlie and Vicki Brown, Lewis Brown, El Wanda and Eddie Horsley, Dee and Billy Hurt, and Charles and Neline Kerr).

Thanks most of all to you, our readers, who we hope will enjoy our stories and pass them on in true Kentucky storytelling tradition.

We were not collectors when we first heard many of these stories, so we did not record the storyteller's name or the time and place of the stories. Some of these stories are based on our own experiences, but many were told to us by more than one person over the years. The tellers included family, neighbors, friends, teachers, and students. In the tradition of storytelling, many of these tales were passed on from generation to generation, with the details often changing slightly with the telling.

We gratefully acknowledge below the individuals who have enriched our lives with the stories they shared, and whose stories we share with you in this book.

John Ackman
Polly Ackman
Edgar Anderson
Iona Anderson
Jerry Anderson
Ervin Atchley
Fatima Atchley

Acknowledgments

Katie Atchley

Cassie Brown

Conda Brown

Lena Brown

Lucian Brown

Sarah Brown

Anna Cravens

Jim Cravens

Mike Dean

Alice Gentry

Charlie Gentry

Hollis Gentry

Geraldine Brown Glascoe

Bob Gutman

Willie Harmon

Zola Harmon

Eva Hughes

Huley Hughes

Ola May (Foley) Martin

Amy Miller

James Milton "Buck" Rooks

George Simpson

Josh Simpson

Lawrence Simpson

Lillian Simpson

Lou Ann (Alley) Simpson

Louis Franklin Simpson

Milt Tom Simpson

Acknowledgments

Sam Simpson
Myrtie Gaskin Sullivan
Leland Voils
Martin Luther Wilson

PART 1
GHOSTS OF SPRING

Springtime is a season filled with wonder. The rebirth of things that have slept through winter makes us marvel at the everlasting cycle of life.

To those of us who grew up in rural south central Kentucky, spring was a time of remembrance and renewal.

Spring brought Easter and the gathering of the community at little Bethlehem Church to celebrate the resurrection of Christ. We put on our Sunday best, not to show off or try to be stylish, but to look our best for this sacred celebration.

Our dead were never forgotten. Dressed in our working clothes, we joined neighbors, relatives, and friends to clear the graveyards that held the bodies of our departed loved ones. On Memorial Day (some called it Decoration Day), we again put on our best and made our way to the graveyards in the community. We put flowers on the graves of family and friends and those who had given their lives for our country, and we stood in silence to honor them. Through the years, it became a traditional reunion. People who had moved away to live and work made a point of coming home. We went to the cemetery to visit the dead and be reunited with the living, whom we had not seen since the last Memorial Day. That custom still continues.

We plowed the fields and planted crops in hopes of a bountiful harvest. With renewed spirits, secure in the knowledge of our place in the universe, we felt a special connection to the souls of those who had crossed over to the other side.

When the day's work was done, we gathered with family and friends after supper to tell stories. If the night was clear and warm, we sat outside on creaking porches or in the yard under the trees, moon, and stars. When gentle rains blanketed the earth or violent spring thunderstorms split apart the sky, we moved inside our houses or even into our storm cellars. On such nights, it was not hard to imagine that spirits from the other side paid us a visit. They showed themselves in the flashes of lightning, they spoke in the rumbles of thunder, and they caressed our faces with the soft touch of the wind and the shadows of the night. Each one in our circle remembered personal encounters to support our belief that there was life beyond the grave. The tradition of storytelling was passed on from generation to generation. One by one, we shared our stories. Believing gave us the strength to move on with our lives, trusting that death was not the end.

If you are looking for scientific proof that ghosts exist, or even an exact definition of what they are, you will not find the answers in this book. This is a collection of true personal experiences and stories we *heard* as true. We will not attempt to convert you to our way of thinking. You must decide for yourself what you believe about ghosts. But whether you believe in ghosts or not, we hope these stories will fill your heart with some of the wonder of Kentucky's eternal springs.

My First Ghost

RB: On a day in early spring when I was seven years old, I had my first personal experience that I could not explain—a paranormal encounter that taught me that love is much stronger than death. I called it "Storm Walker" and included it in my first book, *The Walking Trees and Other Scary Stories* (1991).

The day began like most others. I was walking from our farm to the little one-room school that I attended about a mile away. I didn't mind the walk. Everybody in our neighborhood walked to school. Going to school was a social event that I looked forward to.

There was only one place between home and school that made me shiver and walk a little faster: a thick grove of pines by the side of the dirt road that we called the pine thicket. My mother had convinced me that the owner did not like children; only when I was older did I learn that this man had a moonshine still back in the woods and that my mother had made up the story to keep me away from the men who might be buying the illegal brew. Even though they wouldn't have hurt me, Mom thought they might be drunk and scare me.

The teacher could dismiss school if she thought the weather warranted it. She would let us go early if she saw a storm coming. On those days, I would often meet our neighbor, a man named Jim, who owned the farm next to ours. He would be coming from town and he would walk with me.

Jim would point to hollow trees that he called widow makers. These trees were especially dangerous because the wind or lightning would bring them down and kill the men who took shelter under them. The wives of these dead men became widows, and that is why the trees were called widow makers.

"Never get under a tree in a storm," he'd say. "Get in a gully."

I listened to everything Jim said, but his advice went out of my mind after he developed a heart problem and couldn't walk with me. Treatments for heart patients were very limited then, so the doctor just told Jim to rest. He could no longer take his walks to town or tend the crops in his fields. His three sons were not old enough to work the farm alone, so my father and other neighbors helped them. People looked out for each other in those days.

One night, Dad hurried to get the chores done and Mom rushed to feed us supper and wash the dishes. A heavy black cloud held off just long enough for these tasks to be completed, and then it unleashed a fury of wind, rain, and lightning on our little log house. It did not let up, so after reading a while, we started to prepare for bed. In the midst of loud thunder, we heard a knock at the door. Surprised that anyone would be out in such a raging storm, Dad opened the door to find Jim's two oldest sons, Fred and Carl.

"Dad's worse," Fred said to my father. "Mom says he needs a doctor to draw some fluid from around his heart. Could you go get Mr. Bryant to drive you to town to the doctor's house? She says it's too far for us to go by ourselves."

Mr. Bryant lived on Highway 80 near the school. He was the closest neighbor who had a car. The doctor lived in town, several miles away. Few people had phones in the county, so it was necessary to go into town to get a doctor.

"Go back home and tell your mom that I'm on my way," Dad told the boys. "I'll bring the doctor as soon as I can."

"Thanks," said Carl, and he and his brother turned and hurried for home.

From the window, we could see their lantern bobbing to the end of the lane. As they turned down the dirt road toward their farm, the little light was swallowed up by the trees and the darkness. Dad pulled on his raincoat and disappeared into the storm, too.

Mom sent me to bed, but I couldn't sleep. My friend Jim was seriously ill, and my dad was out in this terrible weather going for help. I knew what it was like to be out in those fields near that pine thicket in storms. It was bad in daylight, but I imagined it would be much worse at night in a violent storm like this. Time dragged by, but I finally fell asleep.

My father was a strong man, but he said later that the wind blew so hard that he had to hold on to small trees and bushes to keep from being blown down. Finally he made it to Mr. Bryant's house, and they brought the doctor to Jim's house. Dad returned home the next morning just as Mom was making breakfast. He said Jim was resting better and would be all right.

Mom and Dad took me to visit Jim often that summer. Jim thanked Dad over and over for going out in the storm to get help for him that night. He said he didn't know how he could ever repay him, but several months later, I think Jim found a way.

On that early spring day, I had no inkling of what was in store for me. An approaching storm led the teacher to dismiss us early, but I was caught in it just as I reached those spooky pines. A tornado developed, and I did not know where to go. Terrified, I took shelter under a single tree by the side of the road. I would have been killed when that tree fell in the storm if Jim had not appeared and led me to safety in a gully back in the pine thicket, a spot that was totally unfamiliar to me. After the storm passed and I reached home, my mother told me that Jim had died two hours before.

My mind had trouble processing the words my mother had just said. I had just seen Jim, and he looked as real as he ever did. I still have no logical explanation for what happened that day. I don't know how a man who had been dead for at least two hours could appear to me and lead me to safety. Maybe his love for children enabled him to reach out from beyond the grave to help me. Maybe saving my life was Jim's way of paying Dad back for going through that horrible storm to get a doctor when Jim desperately needed one.

It really doesn't matter if you think I saw his ghost or if you think it was all in my mind. The result was the same. Jim was able to reach out to me from beyond death and save my life. He was my first ghost.

The Cold Touch

LB: My first brush with the supernatural came when I was very young. My aunt, who had come for a visit, was with me and helped supply details here that I was too young to remember.

The late spring night was sticky hot, a preview of the Kentucky summer that was yet to come. My mom and dad had recently moved us into a one-bedroom house that had once been used as a parsonage near a little country church. Dad boxed off half of the long back porch and made it into a bedroom for me. He added two large windows that allowed the night breezes to blow through and cool the room for good sleeping.

The graveyard beside the church was clearly visible from the window in the back of my room. On the night my aunt came to visit, there was one new grave, completely covered with fresh-cut flowers. The surroundings gave the feeling of peace to those who slumbered.

Since there was only one bedroom in the house, my aunt had the choice of sleeping on the couch or sleeping with me. She decided she would be more comfortable sleeping with me.

"Are you sure?" my mom asked.

"My goodness, yes!" my aunt told her. "With these big windows, this is the coolest room in the house."

Apparently to prove her point, my aunt walked over to the open window and looked out. She was a bit startled by the sight of the new grave in the moonlight.

"Oh, dear," she said, turning to my mother. "There's a new grave! Who was just buried there?"

"You didn't know her," my mother told her. "She and her husband moved here after you went away. Poor thing died in childbirth. Her husband took the baby to his family in Ohio right after the funeral."

"That's such a pity," said my aunt. "Was it a boy or a girl?"

"A boy," my mother answered. "She'd been hoping for a boy, but she never got to see him."

My aunt shook her head, and the conversation ended with our goodnights. Mom and Dad went off to their room, and my aunt and I went to bed. A cool breeze blew through, making the hot night a little more pleasant. My aunt and I drifted off to sleep immediately, but not everything in that serene countryside was resting so peacefully.

I don't know how long we slept, but suddenly we were both awake. Something was in the room with us. I couldn't see anyone, but I could feel a presence. My aunt shivered, and I became very frightened. Then the coldest thing I ever felt in my life touched my shoulder. I cried out at full volume and my aunt reached over to comfort me. As she did that, the cold thing touched her arm, and she began screaming right along with me. Our screams made the thing let go, but fear still had a grip on both of us. We were huddled together when my parents came running in.

"What's the matter?" asked Mom, stopping by the side of the bed.

"Something was in this room," my aunt tried to explain. "I don't know what it was, but I've never felt anything so cold."

"Oh, my goodness!" Mom said, as she sat down on the side of the bed and put her arm around my aunt's shivering shoulders.

"What happened?" Dad asked, lighting the lamp on the bedside table. "Did you see anybody?"

"I didn't see anything," my aunt replied, "but something touched me. It must have touched Lonnie first, because he started crying."

I nodded, still huddled against my aunt.

"It was so cold!" I said. "I don't know what it was!"

"It was something not of this world," my aunt said emphatically. "I've experienced some strange things in my life, but never anything like the thing that was in this room!"

"Well, there's nothing here now," my mother said, trying to soothe us. "Let's try to settle down again and get some sleep."

Mom stood up beside the bed and waited for us to settle down.

Dad crossed to first one window and then the other, looking out to see if anyone was still close by.

"There's nothing in the yard," he said.

He walked back toward the bed to blow out the lamp, but then he stopped and looked down. We watched him bend over and pick something up from the floor.

"How odd," he said, examining the thing he held in his hand. "I wonder how this got in here."

He held it up for us to see in the light from the lamp. We all just stared. What he had picked up from the floor was a fresh funeral flower!

We all tried to go back to sleep, but there was little rest for any of us that night.

We were afraid that there might be more strange happenings, but nothing else came to pay us a visit that night.

My aunt and I never learned what touched us with such an icy hand. We always wondered if that poor, dead mother had come back looking for her baby boy, the son she never got to see. Maybe she just wanted a look at her lost son, or maybe she came back to take him with her. Did she think I was that boy? In any case, I always wondered what might have happened to me that night if my aunt had not been there with me when I encountered my first ghost.

The Night of the Hook Moon

RB: On the night of the hook moon, the sky is inky black except for the moon's little sliver of light. It is curved like a hook and hangs low, maybe waiting, some say, to hook the spirit of a restless soul and pull it back from the grave.

Jim was a believer in the power of the hook moon.

Everybody was surprised when Jim told this story because he didn't seem the sort who could be frightened. But Jim didn't hesitate to admit that this night instilled such fear in him that he was always respectful of the dead after his experience, and he avoided new graves on nights of the hook moon.

That particular night began uneventfully. Jim and his friend Marvin gave little thought to the moon when they mounted their horses and rode down Sano Road to a friend's house to gamble. This was a common practice among Jim's group of friends, even though gambling was frowned on in his little Christian community. On nights when the weather was good and the moon was bright, the men often built a fire outside and gambled by lantern light until dawn. This night was dark because of the hook moon, so a bachelor friend had offered his house to the gamblers for their meeting. To them, it was harmless fun, and a way of picking up a few extra dollars.

The Sano Road ran down a little hill, across a narrow creek that was shallow enough to cross without a bridge, and then up past the Sano Church and graveyard. Deep woods covered several acres behind the church, and the cries of wildcats (called painters or panthers by local people) could be heard at times from those woods at night.

But tonight there was silence. Maybe it was nature's way of paying respect to old Aunt Fetney Ann, whose new grave was beside the road, just inside the graveyard. The silence was the first eerie sign that tonight might be different. Usually Jim and Marvin heard animal sounds as they rode by, and the absence of those sounds tonight made the two men alert to danger.

Aunt Fetney Ann would not have approved of their destination. An avid churchgoer, she always had plenty to say about the evils of gambling and alcohol, and she wasn't shy about saying it to the faces of those who indulged. Most people, including Jim and Marvin, tried to avoid her sharp tongue, but she often cornered them anyway and called them disrespectful. Though death had silenced her, they still felt uncomfortable when they thought of her. If anybody could come back from the grave, it would be Aunt Fetney Ann.

The two men urged their horses on and were relieved when the graveyard was behind them and their friend's house was in view. They quickly forgot the ride by the graveyard as the game began, and money and a jug of moonshine changed hands. By 2:00 A.M., the jug was as empty as their pockets, so Jim and Marvin decided to call it a night.

Their horses plodded steadily down the road, and the thoughts of the two tired riders drifted toward home and bed. Before they realized it, they were once again beside the graveyard and the new grave. Suddenly, in the pale light of the hook moon, something moved beside Aunt Fetney Ann's tombstone, but they could not tell what it was. At the exact same moment, a shattering cry came from the dark woods, and the warm spring air turned cold. The horses reared and neighed as the two men struggled to calm them down.

"What on earth was that?" asked Marvin, still trying to calm his horse. "Did you see it?"

Jim, trying to assure himself that it was nothing to fear, attempted to make light of it as he answered. "Why, that's just old Aunt Fetney Ann chasing a wildcat!"

The words were barely out of his mouth when Jim knew he had made a grave mistake. All at once, something landed on his back and his horse sprang forward at breakneck speed.

Marvin's horse did just the opposite. It reared in the air, came down, and refused to take one step forward. Marvin saw something on Jim's back as the horse raced away, but he couldn't tell what it was. All he could do was try to stay mounted on his own horse as he watched Jim struggle.

Jim tried frantically to rein in his horse and fling the thing off his back at the same time. He succeeded at neither. Bony hands dug into his neck and shoulders, and the musty smell of the earth permeated the air. His breath came in short gasps and he began to feel faint.

Then he saw something ahead that just might be his salvation. It was the little creek that flowed across the road. He had heard that spirits would not cross water, so he held on tightly as his horse entered the stream. At the first splash of water, the ordeal ended. The thing on his back left as mysteriously as it had come. By the time he reined in his horse on the bank of the stream, Marvin had caught up with him.

"Are you all right?" asked Marvin.

"I think so," Jim answered, still gasping for breath.

"My horse was too scared to move," said Marvin. "I never saw anything like it in my life!"

"Me either!" exclaimed Jim. "And I never want to again! I don't know what would have happened if we hadn't come to this stream."

Jim's neck showed bruises for several days, but the whole experience affected him more deeply than the bruises did his skin. It colored his whole way of thinking. He never showed disrespect to the dead again. And when he and Marvin went to other gambling sessions, they never went by the graveyard on the nights of the hook moon. Taking a chance on the hook moon luring Aunt Fetney Ann from her grave again was one gamble Jim didn't ever want to take. He had seen how high the stakes were on that wild night ride, and he knew he didn't have a chance to win.

The Floating Shawl

LB: Little streams in south central Kentucky were often scenes of strange happenings. These sources of water were so important in life that it was only natural that they should play an important part in death. Neighbors gave various accounts of eerie experiences along many of these streams, and though people did not always agree on details, the core of the story was the same. Though the storytellers offered no concrete proof of the things they said they saw and heard, the sincerity in their voices convinced those who listened that the tales were true. Uncle Buck Rooks had such a story to contribute during our story exchanges.

Uncle Buck lived on one of the typical unnamed dirt roads in Adair County. On one side were fields that stretched for miles, and on the other side were thick woods that were always filled with spooky sounds and shadows. The road followed the rise and fall of the rolling hills and was crossed at the bottom of one hill by a small, spring-fed stream.

Near the stream was the cabin where the Smith family—a man, woman, and baby—lived. They had few luxuries, but Mr. Smith had purchased his wife a shawl with a leopard-skin design. She wore it often or used it as a wrap for the baby. She was very proud of it because nobody else had one like it.

One day in late winter, Mr. Smith died after falling from his horse, and Mrs. Smith and the baby were left alone. It was generally known throughout the area that Mr. Smith did not believe in banks and had buried his money somewhere on his land. People assumed that Mrs. Smith and the baby were living off this money.

Winter gave way to early spring, and a group of men decided to meet by the stream, build a fire, and drink and gamble all night. Two men in the group lost heavily. They had been drinking heavily, too, and were not taking their loss very well. When the others in the group left, these two stayed behind and watched the last embers of the fire die out. Neither relished the idea of going home empty-handed, so it was not surprising that they thought of Mr. Smith's buried money. If they could get their hands on it, it would lessen the sting of their loss.

Details of what happened that night differ according to who told the story, but it was generally agreed that the men decided to pay Mrs. Smith a visit and force her to reveal the location of the money. They must have succeeded in finding it, because there was nobody around to help Mrs. Smith resist the drunken gamblers.

In any case, Mrs. Smith and her baby disappeared.

Neighbors later found three sets of footprints near the bank of the stream. There were signs that the earth had been disturbed and the dirt replaced. The two losers suddenly had extra money to spend, but nobody could prove where they had gotten their new wealth. Most people believed that Mrs. Smith wrapped the leopard shawl around her baby and led the men to the buried money.

Explanations of the disappearance of Mrs. Smith and the baby differed. Some said she must have been frightened and left with the baby to live with relatives in some other state. Others thought the worst. They were sure the two drunken men had murdered her and the baby and disposed of the bodies somewhere on the property. There was no proof to support either story, but there were many indications that something sinister had taken place.

Many people passing along the road in both daylight and dark heard a baby crying. So many heard it that the neighbors organized a search party and looked through the Smiths' cabin and all around it. Their efforts turned up nothing, but the baby could still be heard. Some swore they saw shadowy figures moving near the woods at night in the light of the full moon, but nothing of substance was ever found.

Uncle Buck's experience on one warm spring night added another unexplained episode to the mystery. He had traded one of his horses for a retired racehorse. After a couple of days, he decided he needed a bridle for his new horse. He had worked all day, so it wasn't until late afternoon when he rode his racehorse to Grimsley's general store to make his purchase. He found what he wanted and headed home as the last rays of sun were dimming in the sky. It was still light when he came to the stream. Uncle Buck noticed the air grew heavy. He found himself shivering.

Suddenly his horse stopped and refused to move. He gave it a light nudge to get it started, but it still refused to go forward. Then something ahead caught his eye. Out of the stream rose something that looked like a leopard skin! Staring, spellbound, he realized that it was Mrs. Smith's shawl floating over the water. It stayed for a moment, suspended and shimmering, and then disappeared.

The instant it was gone, his horse reared in the air, threw Uncle Buck to the ground, and raced down the road toward home. Uncle Buck brushed himself off and hurried toward home on foot. When he finally arrived home, he found his horse waiting in the barn, still nervous and scared.

Was Mrs. Smith trying to let Uncle Buck know that she and the baby were murdered and their bodies tossed in the stream? The mystery was never solved. No bodies were ever found, and the men were never punished.

The Banshee

RB: My family heritage on both sides (the Simpsons, the Alleys, the Gentrys, and the Deans) is mostly Irish, with a little Scottish sprinkled in. Banshees were common in Irish and Scottish folk stories, and it was natural for some of the stories to be passed down from one generation to the next. The banshee was believed to be real. I don't think I ever heard one; but when the wildcats wailed in the woods near our farm, it was hard to know what to believe.

In Irish folklore, the banshee was a female spirit or fairy who warned of death by wailing. She was also known as the Washer of the Shrouds. Though sometimes described as a young woman, she was more often depicted as an older woman with long hair, which she combed with a silver comb while making her lamentations. One story warns that if you ever see a comb lying on the ground in Ireland, you must never pick it up. If you do, the banshees who placed it there will spirit you away.

Some think of the banshee as a "family spirit" that accompanied Irish families who immigrated to America. The banshee's keening is heard at night prior to a death. Hearing the banshee means a death in the family, but *seeing* the banshee portends one's own death. Upon her arrival, the banshee will remain until the death has occurred. Then she will escort the deceased to the next world.

The banshee stories offered hours of entertainment to the Irish immigrants to Kentucky, but one story was said to be true. Maybe the banshee did indeed come to Kentucky, or maybe the sound in the woods was just an animal. No one can say for sure.

Minnie, a lady who lived on a farm near my great grandmother, was planting her garden one sunny spring day when she suddenly felt weak and dizzy. She leaned for a minute on her hoe until the feeling passed, but she decided she'd better go to the house and rest. Inside, she drank a glass of water and went to lie down, but she began to feel weak and dizzy again. This was not like her. Minnie had always been strong and healthy. Her husband saw her leave the garden and go inside, so he left the field he was plowing to go check on her. She asked him if he would go get my great grandmother Alley. My great grandmother often tended the sick with her herbs when a doctor was not available.

Great Grandmother Alley took her herbs and went along to see what she could do to make Minnie feel better. Minnie felt hot to the touch and complained of a headache that had suddenly come over her. Great Grandmother made some herbal tea and had Minnie drink it, but Minnie didn't improve much. She was tossing and turning from the pain and the fever. Great Grandmother decided that she should stay with her overnight.

Darkness settled in, and Great Grandmother and Minnie's husband were relieved to see Minnie finally settle down. Maybe the herbs were taking effect and bringing relief for the fever and headache. They sat watching her quietly, noticing that her breath seemed to be coming easier now.

Suddenly, the air outside was shattered by a wail like nothing they had ever heard before. Great Grandmother was startled to see that Minnie did not react at all. Her husband, however, turned very pale.

"I am glad I didn't decide to go home alone through

those woods tonight," said Great Grandmother. "I wouldn't want to meet up with that wildcat."

"What you would have met would have been much worse," the husband answered.

"What do you mean?" asked Great Grandmother.

"I mean that was no wildcat," he said.

"What else would make a sound like that?" she asked.

"It was a banshee that wailed," he told her. "It's a sign my Minnie is going to die tonight. Her family has a 'family spirit' that came with them to this country. It has come now to take her to the other side."

"Oh, don't think that!" Great Grandmother told him. "I think she just got too hot working in the garden. She's sleeping now. I think we ought to try to get some sleep, too."

Great Grandmother laid down and drifted off to sleep. She left Minnie's husband sitting by his wife's bed. When she woke, he was still sitting there. She went over to check on Minnie, but Minnie wasn't breathing. Great Grandmother Alley was shocked: Minnie had died during the night.

"Why didn't you wake me?" she asked Minnie's husband.

"There was nothing you could have done," he said. "The banshee came last night to take her away."

Nothing Great Grandmother could say made him change his mind.

Great Grandmother admitted that the cry that night was like nothing she had ever heard, but her practical side had trouble believing in banshees. She looked for signs of wildcats in the woods when she came home later that day, but she found nothing to indicate their presence. Could a wildcat have made such a loud, unearthly sound? Afterward, she always listened for the kind of wailing she had heard the night Minnie died, but she never heard it again.

The stories say that the banshee travels to the homes of those who are going to die sometimes mounted on a pale steed, or riding in a black funeral coach with two headless horses leading the way. Great Grandmother did not see the banshee on a pale steed or headless horses pulling a black funeral coach, but she did see Minnie die from a sudden mysterious illness after the loud wailing in the woods.

In any case, on dark Appalachian nights it might be a good idea to stay inside. What could be out there wailing in the woods? It could just be wildcats and not the banshee, but it wouldn't be pleasant to meet either one.

Shaker Ghost Stories

LB: Not all ghost stories come from other people, or people from the past. Roberta and I have experienced many spooky events of our own in recent times. Shaker Village at Pleasant Hill, Kentucky, is a place that offered us many encounters we could not explain.

We have long been interested in the history of the Shakers. In 2004, we went with our friend Robert Parker (known as Louisville's Mr. Ghost Walker) to tour Shaker Village. At the time, we were interested only in the history of the place; we hadn't read much about the hauntings.

We were told on the tour that the Shakers lived a communal life, practiced celibacy, believed in the equality of the sexes and races, and were staunch pacifists. They got their name from the way they shook during worship services. Persecuted for their beliefs in England, eight Believers and their prophetess leader, Mother Ann Lee, came to America in 1774 and settled near Albany, New York. Within twenty years, eleven Shaker communities had been established in New York and New England. Three Shaker missionaries came to Kentucky in 1800, and by 1825, Pleasant Hill was a thriving community with nearly 500 inhabitants. Their agricultural and manufactured products made the Shaker name a standard of excellence. Unfortunately, the Shakers could not compete with the country's growing industrialization after the Civil War, and the Pleasant Hill settlement officially closed in 1910.

In 1961, a group of private citizens organized to preserve the village and return it to its nineteenth-century appearance. The restored village opened in 1968 and continues as a living history museum today. Even for those who do not believe in ghosts, it is well worth a trip to Pleasant Hill to learn about the Shakers' legacy.

In 2005 our friend Thomas Freese published a book called *Shaker Ghost Stories from Pleasant Hill, Kentucky,* in which he related true accounts of ghostly encounters that were told to him when he worked there as a volunteer. After reading his book, we knew we had to return to Pleasant Hill and tour the place from a haunted perspective. Traveling again with our friend Robert Parker, we booked lodging for March 24, 2006, and set out for a night of adventure.

There is a central dining room at Pleasant Hill, but no central hotel. Guests are put up in rooms in various buildings on the grounds. We had hoped to be near the cemetery where, according to Thomas Freese's sources, a tombstone had once been seen to right itself, but nothing was available in that area. We were assigned to rooms on the second floor of the East Family Sisters' Shop. We soon learned there were enough ghosts to cover all areas.

We arrived at Pleasant Hill in time to have a delicious dinner before settling into our rooms. A cold rain had started falling, but not enough to dampen our enthusiasm. We braved the elements and toured the village, exploring all the places open along Village Pike. A couple of workers shared stories about guests leaving their rooms, only to return to find their door blocked from the inside. Fortunately, that did not happen to us. The rain was coming down harder and the March wind had turned cold, so we were happy to get back inside our rooms without incident and get to bed.

When I turned out the light in our room, we found ourselves in total darkness. The clouds had hidden what light we might have had from the country moon.

"Lonnie," Roberta said, "it's so dark that we'll trip over something if we have to get up during the night. I think I'll turn on the light in the closet by the bathroom and close the door. The little line of light from underneath will act as a night light."

"Good idea," I agreed.

She turned on the light, closed the door, and got back into bed. The little crack of light created the effect we wanted—for a very short while. As we lay there, we noticed that the room was getting lighter and lighter. We looked at the closet and saw that the door was wide open!

"I guess you didn't close it tightly," I said.

"Yeah," she agreed. "I guess I didn't."

She got up, crossed to the closet, and closed the door firmly. "It'll stay closed this time," she said.

She had been back in bed for a couple of minutes when the room grew bright again. We couldn't believe it! Roberta repeated the process of closing the door several times, but it continued to open on its own.

"I give up," said Roberta. "I don't think the Shakers want us to waste electricity!"

When she turned off the light, the door remained closed.

We tried to go to sleep, but the electric clock we had brought from home began to flash. It wasn't a digital clock. It only had a lighted face and dial. It had never flashed before and it has never flashed since, but it flashed that night like a strobe light. It confirmed our belief that the Shakers wanted us to conserve electricity.

When we finally started to doze off, we were awakened abruptly by loud footsteps overhead. Someone was walking above our room.

"I guess they must have rented the room over us to a latecomer," I said to Roberta.

"I guess so," she answered.

The footsteps soon stopped, but I heard them again during the night. I went to sleep and thought no more about it.

The next morning as we were leaving, we were telling Robert about the footsteps. The cleaning lady, who was working in the hallway, heard us.

"Are you talking about here at this place?" she asked.

"Yes," I told her. "Someone must have come in late. We heard them walking in the room over us."

"That's not possible," she told us. "Let me show you."

She produced a large ring of keys from her pocket and went up the stairs to the door above our room. She opened the door and invited all of us to look inside. We were amazed to see that it wasn't a room they rented out at all. It was a small storage area not nearly big enough for someone to walk around, yet we had both heard the footsteps.

After breakfast, we began a self-guided tour of the entire village. Overnight, the rain had turned to light snow, giving the entire village a look of enchantment. We were quiet as we approached the door of the Meeting Hall. This was the place where the Shakers had held their worship services and had done their whirling dances. I was in front, with Roberta and Robert close behind. I pulled the door open and, before we could blink, the three of us were engulfed in a strong whirlwind coming out the door! It was so strong that it raised our hair, and then it disappeared as suddenly as it had come. We were startled, but we went inside anyway. We must have met the dancing spirits going out. Later, we heard other accounts of similar experiences with the whirlwind.

For the best information about Shaker ghosts, buy Thomas Freese's book, *Shaker Ghost Stories from Pleasant Hill, Kentucky,* available in bookstores, from amazon.com, and from Thomas's Web site, thomaslfreese.com.

A Doctor in the House

RB: This story is incredible, but true. It is a matter of public record, but out of respect for some of the parties who are still alive, I am using only first names.

It was Sunday morning, May 25, 1969. I was drying my hair so I could go out later when my new hair dryer stopped working for no reason. I spent the next hour or so looking for my old dryer and using it to finish drying my hair.

Then the phone rang. I thought it would be a friend wanting to chat. I never dreamed it would be a call telling me that one of my best friends, Jane, had been brutally murdered.

When I heard the news, I couldn't believe it. I had gone from Louisville to Cincinnati to visit her just a couple of weeks before, and she had given me the new hair dryer as a special gift. I learned later that the dryer stopped that morning at the exact time of her death.

At the end of that last visit, Jane followed me out to the car, telling me over and over that we needed to visit more often. I have wondered since then if she had a premonition of her coming death.

"We never see each other as much as we should. Life is too short! Come back soon," she said.

I agreed and drove away, leaving her standing in the driveway of her family's new home in Cincinnati. It was the last time I ever saw her alive.

The caller who gave me the devastating news was a mutual friend, Grace, from the Kentucky college I had attended. I was dazed as I listened to the gruesome details.

Grace and I had both worked with Jane, who was a psychiatrist at the college health service. Jane and her husband, Charles, a dean at the college, knew I needed money for college expenses, so they asked me to move into their house as a live-in babysitter for their two young children. It turned out to be one of the most rewarding experiences of my life. They treated me like a member of the family.

When I first moved into their home, I was reluctant to let them know about my interest in the supernatural. Because Jane was a psychiatrist, I thought that if I told her about my belief, she might think I was too crazy to take care of her children. Eventually I got the courage to share a strange experience I'd had, and I found Jane very open and willing to accept the idea of paranormal events. In fact, she gave me material to read on the latest research being done at the time at Duke University.

The year I graduated from college, Jane and Charles adopted a seventeen-year-old girl named BJ. Charles retired and they moved to Cincinnati so Jane could complete a residency and establish a practice from an office in the basement of their home.

"I've given this serious thought," Jane told me, "and I think this is the best thing to do. Charles is much older than I am and he's likely to die before I do, probably when the children are at an age to need me most. By having my office at home, I can be there for them. It will help to have BJ in the house, too."

Sadly, as things turned out, Jane was almost totally wrong.

It was in this house in Cincinnati on that May morning that Jane was shot four times and beaten nineteen times with a poker. From information gathered in the subsequent investigation, it was established that Charles and the two children went to Sunday school, leaving Jane at home with plans to do the laundry and join them for the church service later. BJ elected to go horseback riding some fifteen miles away at the riding stables that she frequented. Jane never made it to church. Someone entered the house and viciously ended her life. Her thirteen-year-old son came home first and found her dead on the floor of her office. The rest of the family arrived soon after, stunned at what was waiting for them.

As I hung up from Grace's call that terrible Sunday morning, I immediately dialed Jane's number in Cincinnati. I found myself talking to a Detective Jackson, who was chief of the homicide bureau of the Cincinnati Police Department. He quizzed me intensely about who I was, where I was, and what connection I had to the family. Satisfied with my answers, he finally let me talk to Charles.

In the days that followed, we were all to receive more shocks. BJ, the adopted daughter, who was then twenty-three and still living at home, was arrested and charged with Jane's murder. At first she told investigators that she had last seen Jane alive about 9:30 A.M., when she left to go riding. A search of her locker at the riding stables turned up blood-spattered boots. At that point, BJ confessed to the murder, then later recanted the confession. She said she gave a false confession because she was afraid the police might blame Jane's husband, Charles, and she didn't want the children to lose both parents.

In spite of BJ's withdrawn confession, the police put together a case strong enough to convict her. She tried to commit suicide after the sentencing, but the attempt failed. BJ served twenty years in prison for the murder.

During their investigation, police learned that Jane and BJ had been having screaming arguments over BJ's pet monkey and a boyfriend of whom Jane did not approve. There were other problems, too. It appeared that the two of them must have been arguing that Sunday morning in an upstairs bedroom as Jane was getting ready to take a shower. Jane likely walked away in an attempt to end the conflict, but BJ followed and fired the first shot through a pillow to muffle the sound.

As Jane tried to escape downstairs, BJ must have followed her, firing the fatal shots. Perhaps Jane grabbed the poker in self-defense, but was unable to use it. It was found lying across Jane's right arm. The killer evidently used it to beat her, then wiped it clean of prints.

Before the trial began, I followed the investigation in disbelief. The home I had shared with this family was loving, peaceful, and organized. Jane had a place for everything and expected it to be there. "I want to be able to reach in a drawer in the dark and put my hand on exactly what I need!" she would say.

When I moved into my own apartment, I organized my silverware drawer the way Jane did. But in the days right after her murder, I would get up in the morning and find my silverware in complete disarray. Being the only one living in the apartment, I thought maybe Jane was trying to let me know that her spirit lived on and that she was okay despite all that had happened.

Jane came to me again in a dream, or perhaps a visitation, one night shortly after I noticed the silverware. I had just gone to bed when she appeared to me. She looked as real as she had looked in life. We talked like we used to when I lived with her and her family.

"Everything has changed so much!" she told me. "You would not believe that we are the same people. You are going to hear some very shocking details about our lives during the upcoming trial. I just wanted to prepare you."

The trial proved her right. I *was* shocked! From the trial testimony I learned that Jane and Charles were considering a separation and that Jane had told BJ she would have to move out.

Jane's memorial service brought me little solace. I had often turned to Jane for advice, and now she was gone. I missed her very much. Many times I caught myself reaching for the phone to discuss something with her. I kept in touch with Jane's family, and was happy to find that, over time, they were able to deal with their grief and move on. I tried to do the same.

I had no more dreams or visits from Jane until a year after the trial. The lease on my current apartment would soon be up, and I was thinking seriously about renting an apartment from some friends on Belgravia Court in downtown Louisville. It was a great neighborhood for artists and writers, and I knew several people who lived in the area. The rent was affordable, and the apartment was close to theaters and stores. I finally made up my mind, and I went to bed that night thinking I would call my friends the next day and tell them that I wanted to rent the place.

Then a strange thing happened. Jane came that night to visit me again. She looked very worried. It seemed as though she was actually there with me in the room when she began to speak.

"I don't think you should move," she told me. "Something bad is going to happen there, and if you move, you will be involved."

This was not what I wanted to hear, because I really liked the apartment downtown and wanted to start moving in right away. Jane's advice was so strong in my mind, however, that I decided to wait a week or so to call my friends and give them my decision. It was a good thing that I listened to Jane.

The next week, I got the news that burglars had broken into the house where I had thought of moving. One of my friends was in the hallway at the time of the break-in and was shot by one of the intruders. My friend nearly died and had to undergo several surgeries and many months of painful rehabilitation. He was in a common entrance hall at the time of the shooting. Had I rented that apartment, I could have been in the hallway and I could have been the one shot.

Charles died a few years after Jane's death, and I lost touch with their children. I never tried to contact BJ, either while she was in prison or after she was released. When I thought about making contact, Jane's face would pop into my mind and she would shake her head. I decided that Jane's advice was worth taking.

The Thing in the Woods

LB: Workdays in the spring were especially long on our small Kentucky farm. The ground had to be plowed, and the crops had to be planted and tended. Maybe the extra chores and the extra time spent doing them made my parents forget to buy oil for the lamps. Whatever the reason, we often ran out, and I was the one chosen to take the oil can to Sullivan's store and get the oil we needed. I wouldn't have minded if this request had come mid-morning or mid-afternoon so I could take a break from my chores, but it never came then. It always came just before dark as we were leaving the fields so Mom could fix supper.

"Hon, run to the store for me and get some oil," Mom would say to me.

On this particular day, Dad reached in his pocket and pulled out just enough money to pay for it and then he said, "Hurry, son! The woods will be dark soon."

I knew that well enough. I tried to avoid being in those woods alone after dark because of the stories I'd heard. There was an old abandoned house in there, the old Burton place, which was said to be haunted. Once, when my friend Jerry and I had cut through the woods at night on our way home from a friend's house, we had seen a light moving back and forth through the broken windows. We went back the next day, but we found no evidence that any human had been inside. Stories persisted that the ghost of old Mr. Burton roamed the woods at night looking for whoever murdered him years and years before. I knew I shouldn't worry because that had nothing to do with me, but I still felt uneasy walking through the woods alone.

There was no use in taking the lantern because there was no oil in it, but I thought I'd feel better if I at least had the company of our dog, Brownie. We only made it to the edge of the yard when Dad called Brownie back.

"You'll play too much if that dog's along," he called.

Some rays of the afternoon sun were still making it through the trees as I started along the path to the store. Trees still looked like trees at that point. Later, the shadows would make them look like monstrous forms reaching for me. I knew Mr. Sullivan would open the store for me because his house stood right beside it, but I hoped he wouldn't talk long that night. He always loved to visit with his customers.

I came out of the woods and saw the store ahead of me. I had a bit of luck, because I could see the door was still open. I made my purchase and was relieved when another customer came in just as I was finishing. Mr. Sullivan started talking to him, so I could make my escape.

Sunlight had dimmed to a glow as I stepped into the woods and headed home. The darkness that had already settled way back in the woods now came creeping toward me. By the time I was a third of the way home, I could hardly see the path. The old Burton place was to my right, and I looked in its direction from the corner of my eye. For an instant, I thought I saw something move, but I told myself it was nothing.

Then I heard it. Something was walking along the path behind me. I stopped, and it stopped too. I started again, walking a little faster, and it kept pace with me. It couldn't be the other customer at Mr. Sullivan's store; he lived in the other direction. It couldn't be my friend Jerry trying to scare me because he didn't know I was out there. It couldn't be Mr. Burton's ghost. There were no such things, were there? My mind raced to identify the thing in the woods behind me.

"Brownie!" I said to myself, relieved to have come up with such a satisfactory answer. "He must have followed me after all."

I stopped again.

"Brownie?" I called, but there was no response.

I walked on with my spirits lifted, even though the footsteps behind me did not sound exactly like a dog's footsteps. Ahead was a slight bend in the path, with a big rock right by the side. It was very dark at that spot now. The footsteps behind me came closer and closer, faster and faster. Just as I neared the rock, something touched my back. I froze for an instant without moving forward another inch. My entire system was shut down by fear.

"Brownie has just jumped on me like he does when he wants to play," I told myself.

But the touch did not feel like Brownie's paws. It felt more like hands holding me, preventing me from moving forward. I became aware of complete silence all around me except for one sound. It was a rattle coming from the middle of the road near the rock. It had to be a rattlesnake! In another minute, I would have stepped on it and it likely would have bitten me. My body revived, and I moved back a few steps. As I heard the snake slither off the path toward the rock, I realized nothing was touching me now. I whirled around, but nothing was behind me. Everything was quiet, but it was a peaceful stillness now. The thing in the woods couldn't have been Brownie because there was nothing on the path with me now.

I hurried as fast as I could, and I was breathless, but happy, when I emerged from the woods to see our house. Brownie was sleeping on the front porch.

"Has he been here the whole time since I left?" I asked.

"Yes," said Dad. "He hasn't moved."

I never figured out what followed me and stopped me in the woods that night. I made many more trips to Mr. Sullivan's store, but none had a supernatural touch. I wonder if the thing could still be down in the woods of Kentucky, waiting to help some other traveler on a dark and spooky night.

Waiting on the Stairs

RB: One day, after months of dealing with contractors and builders, my friend Etta called me to give me the good news that their new house was finally finished.

"I am so glad we got to move in this spring," she said. "I've already started planting flowers and shrubs. You've got to come over and stay for the weekend. We'll have a house-warming."

It sounded like a good idea, so I accepted Etta's invitation. I threw some things into an overnight bag and drove to her house.

The house was located off Old Third Street Road in Louisville in a quiet, lovely neighborhood. I certainly didn't expect to get into a shoving match with a dead person as soon as I arrived!

I was admiring the elegance of the carved banister and the plush-carpeted stairs as Etta led me up to the second-floor guest room. As we neared the top of the stairs, something—or someone—got between my friend and me. I saw nothing, but I definitely sensed a presence there facing me. I couldn't move, even though Etta had already reached the second-floor hallway and was waiting for me. I suddenly felt a cold touch, and I was pushed so hard that I had to grab the banister to keep from falling.

"Are you all right?" Etta asked. "Are you dizzy?"

"No," I told her. "Something pushed me!"

"It couldn't have! I've been standing right here looking at you and I only saw you," she said. "You must have tripped on the carpet."

"No, I didn't," I insisted. "You've got a ghost! I've got a feeling that somebody died on these stairs!"

"Roberta," she said patiently, "that's impossible. Nobody has ever lived in this house but us, and we are all alive! So don't start about ghosts!"

Her reasoning didn't convince me. I knew that there was something in that house that was not of this world, and I knew it was waiting for me when I came to the top of the stairs. I felt so strongly that this invisible being was going to push me again that I actually sat down and scooted my way up and down the stairs when I needed to get to the second floor for the rest of my visit. My friend thought it was hilarious; still, I felt relieved when my visit ended.

A few weeks later, Etta called, bubbling with excitement.

"I guess I owe you an apology," she said.

"Why?" I asked her.

"You'll never believe what I heard at the beauty shop today," she said. "An old lady who used to live nearby came in and began talking about the old days. When she found out where I live, she said, 'Honey, did you know there used to be a house exactly where yours is? A woman died on the stairs there years ago. Nobody ever knew if she fell or was pushed, but it was odd that her husband married a younger woman right away and moved out of town.'"

"I am not surprised," I told her. "I was telling the truth, but I know you thought I was nuts."

"I'm sorry I didn't believe you," she said.

Etta moved away soon after that because of a job change, so I don't know if the ghost is still on the stairs. When I recall that ghost now, I don't think she meant to hurt me. I believe she just wanted someone to know she was murdered. I hope that her showing me that she was pushed brought her peace. Sometimes to know and care is all it takes to release an earthbound spirit and send it to the light. I hope that is true in her case and that she is no longer waiting on the stairs.

Outline in Blood

RB: Katie and Rufus moved into an old Kentucky farmhouse in early spring. They were surprised and delighted to have found the place, because the rent was very reasonable. In fact it was quite low, considering the good condition of the house. With the house came several acres of land, on which Rufus planted corn and tobacco and Katie planted a vegetable garden. Soon the crops and the vegetables began to grow, and Katie and Rufus began to think that they had a good deal indeed.

One night, Rufus and Katie had gone to bed after a hard day of working on their little farm when something woke them from a deep sleep. A sharp crack and a thud sounded from the yard just outside their window. Someone cried out in pain, and then all was silent.

"What was that?" Katie asked, sitting up in bed.

"It sounded like a gunshot," Rufus said, sitting up beside her and swinging his feet to the floor. "I'm going to check it out."

"You can't go out there!" Katie protested. "Somebody just got shot!"

"All the more reason for me to check," Rufus answered. "Somebody might be hurt and need help."

"Look out first and see if anybody's out there," suggested Katie. "It sounded like it came from near the clothesline."

Rufus took her advice and looked out all the windows. The full moon lit up the yard, but Rufus could see absolutely nothing out of place. He stepped out the back door and then out the front door, but nothing unusual met his eye. He gave up the search and went back to bed.

"Maybe we were dreaming," he suggested.

"I hardly think we would both have the same dream," replied Katie. "It was definitely real!"

In the morning, Katie was up early and had her wash ready to hang on the line by sunup. She and Rufus started to the clothesline with two baskets of wet clothes. She liked to smell the fresh scent of the outdoors when they were dry, so she liked to hang them early in the morning sun. Katie was walking a few steps ahead of Rufus when she saw it. She dropped the basket and screamed.

"What's the matter?" Rufus asked, trying to see what had frightened her.

Katie was pointing to the ground directly ahead of them. Rufus set his basket down and looked over her shoulder toward the clothesline where she was pointing. Neither could believe what they were seeing. On the ground was the outline of a body in blood!

Katie was too shaken to continue. She ran into the house crying. Rufus hung the clothes and joined her inside. They decided to go straight down to Conover's old country store and report what they had heard and seen. Mr. Conover had a phone, so they could call the sheriff.

Mr. Conover listened to their story, but he didn't seem too surprised.

"Somebody should have warned you," he told them. "I figured old man Leach told you what happened before he rented you the place. He hasn't lived there since it happened. He moved in with his son, and he just rents the place out for whatever he can get for it."

"What happened?" Rufus asked. "Tell us!"

"It's been several years," Mr. Conover told them. "Mr. Leach had been losing chickens, and he thought that maybe there was either a low-down chicken thief or a fox that was catching them. One night he heard his chickens making an awful ruckus, so he grabbed his gun and fired into the dark. He heard a cry, and he knew he had shot the thief. But it wasn't a thief or a fox. It was just a young neighbor boy who was cutting through Mr. Leach's yard on his way home from visiting his girlfriend."

"How horrible!" said Katie.

"Yes, it was," Mr. Conover continued. "No charges were brought against Mr. Leach because the young man was on his property, but Mr. Leach never got over it. He couldn't stand to stay there after that. He moved and started renting the place out."

"But what about what we saw?" asked Katie. "I don't understand why the body was outlined in blood."

"Every year on the anniversary of that tragic event, it's acted out all over again," explained Mr. Conover. "Renters hear the gunshot and hear the young man cry out. In the morning, they see what you saw. An outline of the body of the young man appears in blood right where he fell and bled to death. It disappears by the end of the day, though. Don't worry now. You won't see it again until next spring."

At the end of the day, the bloody outline was gone, just as Mr. Conover said it would be. Before the next spring, Katie and Rufus had gone, too. Maybe that tragedy is still replayed every spring, but Katie and Rufus didn't want to be around on the next anniversary to find out.

Murder Replayed

RB: A man named Blevins was driving home from a business trip when a strong spring thunderstorm hit. He had taken a shortcut down a two-lane road that was not familiar to him, and now he realized that he had not made a wise decision. He leaned forward, trying to see the road, but the rain was coming down too fast for the windshield wipers to clear it away.

He barely saw the narrow, roaring stream rushing across the road ahead of him in time to apply his brakes and stop. He sat there, shaken and disgusted with himself for getting into such a situation. He had no idea how deep the stream was or how strong the current might be. He couldn't take a chance of trying to cross and getting swept away. He would have to wait until morning to continue safely.

As Blevins sat, wondering how he would sleep all cramped up in his car, a flash of lightning revealed an old house just a short distance from the road. The place looked deserted, but Blevins thought he would be more comfortable in a space large enough to stretch out and move around than he would be in his car. He grabbed his umbrella and the blanket he kept in a plastic bag for emergencies and made a dash from the car to the house.

He was right about the place being deserted. The door creaked as he closed it behind him, but at least it kept out the wind and rain. His eyes adjusted as he looked around when the lightning flashed. There was a fireplace with some wood, and he quickly managed to get a fire going. He looked around the room and saw an old chair that turned out to be quite sturdy. He pulled it close to the fire, sat down, and wrapped himself in the blanket while he waited for the fire to banish the chill from the empty house.

The storm intensified, and Blevins began to get sleepy. He was almost dozing off when the front door suddenly creaked open and a man walked in. He was carrying a dead boy over his shoulders. Totally ignoring Blevins, the man walked to the center of the room and dropped the boy's body on the floor. It immediately disappeared, as if the floor had opened up and let him drop through. Without a word of acknowledgment to Blevins, the man turned and left by the front door.

Blevins immediately jumped up and went to the spot where the body had been, thinking maybe there was a trap door in the floor. Nothing was there. Puzzled and a little frightened, he sat down again in the chair. A few minutes passed, and the door creaked open again. The same man entered, this time carrying a dead woman across his shoulders. Again he dumped the body in the middle of the floor and left without a word or a look in Blevins's direction. The woman vanished just as the boy had done.

Blevins again got up and looked at the floor, but there was no opening of any kind. Shaken, he sat in the chair, expecting another visit. His instinct was to run for help, but he was reluctant to go out in the storm. Time passed slowly and nothing else happened. Exhausted, Blevins finally fell sleep.

When he woke, the storm was over and the sky had cleared. He hurried down to his car and could see in the daylight that there was a little bridge across the stream where he had stopped the night before. The water had covered it then, but now the water had receded and left the bridge exposed. He took a close look and could detect no damage, so he took a chance and drove across. A few miles down the road, he came to a small town. He went directly to the sheriff's office.

The sheriff poured Blevins a cup of strong, hot coffee and listened to his story. He nodded his head when he finished.

"I know the old house," the sheriff said. "A man who lived there years ago killed his wife and son and hid their bodies under the floor. It's strange, but I think you must have experienced a time warp or something and ended up watching a replay of the murder. We found the bodies under the middle of the floor just where you said he dropped them. Mr. Blevins, you must have seen their ghosts."

Burn My Chair

LB: My Aunt Shirley loved to go to dances when she was young. She was a good dancer, and her dance card was always filled. Every young man in the county loved to whirl her around on the dance floor. She was a sight to see when Great Uncle Coy's carriage pulled up and let her out at local parties.

Then one night, it all ended suddenly. Coy was driving Shirley home from the annual May Day dance. A noise from the bushes beside the road spooked the horses, and they jerked the carriage as they took off running along the bumpy road. Shirley was thrown from the carriage and her lovely dancing gown caught in the wheels. She was dragged and thrown against a large rock as Coy frantically fought the horses to a halt.

He rushed to Shirley, who was crying out.

"I can't move my legs," she sobbed. "I can't move!"

Coy lifted Shirley into the carriage and drove home. He and her mother put her to bed and sent for the doctor.

"I am sorry," the doctor said as he finished his examination. "I'm afraid the condition is permanent. It would take a miracle for her to walk again."

No miracle was forthcoming. Shirley tried, but her legs would not work. In despair, the family had to accept the fact that there would be no more dancing for Shirley. She would be crippled for life. In an effort to help, Coy bought his daughter a wheelchair, but she hated it.

Shirley began to waste away. She sat in the chair every day and got weaker and weaker. Soon May approached again, but Shirley would not dance this May Day. She would sit this one out in her wheelchair.

"Burn this chair when I die!" she said to her father. "I don't want this thing to survive when I'm gone. Burn it, do you hear?"

Coy promised to do as his daughter wished. That would be a long time in the future, he thought. But he was wrong. Shirley died quietly in the chair one day soon after she got her father to make the promise.

No one thought about the wheelchair during Shirley's funeral. When Coy came home after the service and saw it, he remembered the promise he had made to his daughter. It seemed a shame, though, to burn a perfectly good wheelchair. Maybe someone else would need it sometime. He decided to keep it at the house until he could talk to the doctor in town. Maybe the doctor would know of someone to give it to. Coy pushed the chair into the corner of Shirley's room.

That night, the family sat on the porch in silence, grieving. Shirley had been so full of life before the accident. Why had it ended this way?

Then suddenly Coy jumped to his feet.

"I smell smoke," he said, running into the house.

His wife followed closely behind him as he rushed to Shirley's room. He opened the door. Smoke and flames greeted them from the corner of the room.

"My Lord!" his wife gasped. "The chair is on fire!"

Coy grabbed a quilt and tried to smother the flames. His wife ran to the kitchen for a bucket of water. She returned and threw water on the chair, but it continued to burn. The odd thing was that the fire did not spread. It seemed to be self-contained in the wheelchair. Helpless, the couple watched as the fire burned itself out. As the flames died down, a strange thing happened. The smoke took the shape of a young woman, and it whirled round and round as if it were dancing. Then it disappeared.

Julie's Return

RB: My sister Fatima told us about her first memory of a supernatural happening from the spring when she was five or six years old. This is the story she shared with us.

We lived next door to my Aunt Zola's family, and my cousin Julie, who was several years older than I was, used to play with me. I thought Julie was just about perfect, with her long red hair and unending patience with me. We would lie on our backs in the grass, look at the sky, and indulge in our favorite pastime of cloud watching. We saw all sorts of things up there, but the forms would change and move away.

In the late spring, my parents decided to move to Cincinnati, Ohio, so Dad could find work. I was devastated. I did not want to leave Julie.

"I don't want to move away. We won't ever see each other again!" I told Julie as we said good-bye.

"Oh, Fatima, sure we will!" she assured me, giving me a hug. "We'll see each other again. I promise!"

That was a comfort to me because Julie always kept her promises.

I missed Julie a lot, but I adjusted to life in Cincinnati. I had cousins and friends to play with there.

Then, in late fall, Aunt Zola sent us a letter saying Julie was ill. The doctor said she had tuberculosis, a lung disease that was almost always fatal in those days. Aunt Zola was not only concerned for Julie's physical welfare, but she was concerned for her spiritual welfare as well. Julie had professed her belief in Christ at a revival meeting in the little country church her family attended, but Julie was not baptized with the other converts. The baptism was held in Russell Creek, and since the air had turned chilly, the doctor did not think Julie should be outside soaking wet in a creek in her condition. It seemed wiser to wait until spring.

However, by the time the next spring came, Julie was dead. My aunt overheard some older women in the neighborhood wondering about the state of Julie's soul, and she began to worry. Was Julie happy in the next life, or was she in torment?

Mom and Dad returned to Russell County for Julie's funeral, but they did not take me. They didn't talk about it to me, either, because they thought I was too young to understand. I knew Julie was dead, but I really didn't know what it meant to be dead.

Soon after the funeral, Mom and Dad decided not to go back to Cincinnati, so we moved back into our old house. I was sad because Julie was not there to play with me this spring like she had before.

One warm, sunny day, I went outside to play by myself. I lay down in the grass on my back and began to look at the sky, like Julie and I used to do. My attention was drawn to three small, white, fluffy clouds drifting across the otherwise clear sky. They stopped just overhead, and the middle cloud changed into a coffin. I was so young, I didn't know what it was. I called it a big box with a lid.

Fascinated, I watched the long lid open slowly, and then I saw someone sit up. I was delighted to see that it was Julie! She leaned over the side, smiled down at me, and waved. She was wearing a white dress with a blue bow, and her long red hair hung over her shoulder. She was fingering a locket with one hand. I had never seen her look so happy.

I remember that we communicated by thoughts.

Come play with me, Julie! I said to her.

I'd love to, she answered, *but I have to go. I just wanted to come see you again like I promised.*

Julie waved again, lay back in the coffin, and the lid closed. It turned back into a cloud again, and the three clouds drifted on across the sky.

I scrambled to my feet and ran inside. Breathlessly, I told my mother what had just happened.

"You just thought you saw her," Mom said, but she had a puzzled look on her face when I described what Julie was wearing. I had described Julie's funeral dress, but nobody had told me anything about that.

"Don't say anything about this to your Aunt Zola," Mom warned me sternly. "It will just upset her."

I made no promise because I could hardly wait to tell Aunt Zola about seeing Julie in the sky. I blurted it out as soon as I saw her.

"Hush!" said my mother, but Aunt Zola told Mom to let me talk. When I finished, Aunt Zola had tears in her eyes, but she was smiling.

"I'm glad you told me," she said. "Now I won't worry anymore."

In those days, when someone died, they were dressed and laid out at home, usually in a homemade coffin. After the neighbors came in to pay their respects, the corpse was taken to the graveyard and buried.

"Before they took Julie out," Aunt Zola continued, "I had a few minutes alone with her. I took her favorite locket and placed it around her neck out of sight under the blue bow. I knew the undertakers did not like for people to be buried with jewelry because of stories about grave robbers, so nobody but me knew she was buried with the locket you saw. I won't worry now. I know that somewhere she exists and is happy."

Grandmother's March

RB: Fatima had another eerie story that she told us.

Grandmother Simpson always said, "If I live through March, I'll live another year."

Grandmother and I were very close, so I was always relieved to see March come and go. When that happened, I knew I'd have Grandmother another year, because I never doubted what she said.

After I grew up, I married and moved to Nashville, and Grandmother's final March eventually came. She was living with her son, my Uncle Josh, at Glasgow, Kentucky, and was sick for several months before she died in March of 1958. We visited her often while she was sick, but she didn't seem any worse than usual the last Sunday we were there.

At 2:00 A.M. on Friday, a week before she died, something woke me in my home in Nashville. At first I thought it was our furnace, which sometimes made a popping sound when it cut on or off. Fully awake, I listened and heard the distinct, shuffling footsteps of my grandmother. I lay awake the rest of the night listening to her slow march through my house, although at the time I knew she was ill in bed over one hundred miles away.

The next day, my husband went to work and my son went to school, but I was not alone. Grandmother's footsteps continued, even though it was bright daylight. Late that afternoon, we got word that she had gotten much worse at 2:00 A.M., but had rallied before my uncle called us.

The next Friday morning, I was alone in the house washing dishes when I heard the footsteps start again. This time they were right behind me everywhere I went in the house. I did not actually hear her call my name, but I knew she was trying to get my attention. I knew without a doubt that I must go to Grandmother at once if I wanted to see her alive.

I packed our bags and was ready to go when my husband and son got home. My husband tried to talk me into waiting until Saturday morning.

"I'm tired," he said. "You know how horrible Friday afternoon traffic is in Nashville. Can't we wait and drive up in the morning?"

"No!" I insisted. "We have to go tonight! I have to see her."

He gave in, and we drove to Glasgow.

When we got there, I was not surprised to find that Grandmother had taken a turn for the worse. She had been hurting and yelling so loudly that she could be heard as far as the road outside the house. My uncle and aunt had been debating whether to call me or not because I had never been able to deal with suffering like that. I also had a horror of death, so they didn't know what to do. Then, just before we arrived, they told me, Grandmother had stopped yelling and gone into a deep sleep.

When she woke, she was in pain, but was peaceful. I sat by her bed and heard her describe the beautiful things and places she was seeing. She spoke to friends and relatives who had died before.

She looked at me and said, "Turn me loose, child, and let me go!"

Grandmother died at 2:00 A.M. that March morning. Watching her cross over was a blessing for me. Since then, I no longer have a horror of death.

Clifford's Death

RB: One of the strangest experiences my sister Fatima had was this one.

One day in May 1958, my husband, son, and I were having lunch at our home when a terrible sadness suddenly came over me. I heard someone take a step on gravel, slip, and fall. My husband noticed the strange look on my face and asked what was wrong.

"I just heard a man slip and fall on gravel," I replied. "I see him. He's in Indiana. He fell on his face and he's dead."

We tried to think of whom we might know in Indiana, but nobody came to mind. Our relatives lived in Kentucky and Ohio. We had forgotten that my uncle, aunt, and cousins had just moved to a farm in Indiana across the state line from Harrison, Ohio. We had never been there.

A few hours later, we got a call and were told that my

cousin Clifford, who lived on that Indiana farm, had been accidentally killed. He had just been discharged from the army and was suffering from some blood pressure problems. Clifford's dad and his best friend, Chris, were target practicing with him in the backyard. Clifford stood up, took a step, and pitched forward as his foot slipped on gravel. Maybe his blood pressure had made him dizzy. In any case, he staggered into the line of fire just as his friend pulled the trigger. He fell face down and died instantly.

I kept insisting that Clifford must have slipped on some gravel, but the family insisted that there was only grass back there. When my mother went for the funeral, she looked in the backyard where the accident had happened. The yard was mostly grassy, but an old driveway had once circled the area. There was still a small patch of gravel where the old driveway had been.

When we calculated the time difference between our house and the Indiana farm, we realized that I had had that vision of the accident precisely when it actually occurred.

PART II
GHOSTS OF SUMMER

The Chivaree

Kentuckians' penchant for storytelling extended into the hot months of summer. During the day, most people worked their crops. For the few who were not working the fields, there were favorite places to gather and tell stories. Women would sit on the porch or under a shade tree while they peeled apples or peaches or broke beans to can, and would share stories to make the work go faster. Men might gather on the town square or at the local country store to whittle with their old pocketknives and pass the time by telling tales.

Summer campfires, front porches, and backyard fire pits were also sites for spinning yarns. The boiling black clouds of summer storms added the perfect backdrop. The listeners and storytellers may have scurried inside for shelter, but they continued to share stories, giving accounts of being caught out in storms and encountering ghostly beings whose rest in the grave had been disturbed by the thunder and howling wind.

There was no air conditioning, so on stormy nights, doors and windows were left open so the fresh air could circulate through the house. Unexplained night sounds came through with the breeze and made people wonder if ghosts were drawing near to join their storytelling circle. Lamplight cast sinister shadows and caused people to draw closer to each other. Those stories brought a warmth to the heart that was different from the summer heat.

The House That Didn't Like People

RB: There was nothing sinister about the way the house looked when my brother-in-law, Ervin, and my sister, Fatima, first saw it. It was a typical, modern, three-bedroom house with a long front porch, located not too far from the Tennessee-Kentucky state line. There was a two-car garage just off the master bedroom and a circular drive that wound through the rolling lawn in the back. Bordering the back lawn was a little creek with woods on the opposite bank. The neighborhood seemed quiet and orderly.

Fatima and Ervin were exhausted from house-hunting all day. They had to find something right away, and this house looked perfect. Best of all, it was well within their budget.

As they were walking through the house, Fatima stopped and said to Ervin, "This house doesn't like people!"

Fatima often had "feelings" like this, so it was not unusual for her to make such a remark. It was not what Ervin wanted to hear. His new job started in three days, and they had no more time to look. They needed to move in right away and get settled.

"There is nothing wrong with this house," he told his wife patiently. "I think we ought to take it."

After some discussion, Fatima decided to ignore her feelings and go ahead with the deal. Thus began some of the strangest years of our lives.

After they moved into the house, I often spent my summer vacations there when I was not in school. Right away, we all began to realize that there was something in the house that had not moved out when Ervin and Fatima moved in. It wasn't long until we knew Fatima had been right. The house didn't like people!

The first puzzling thing we noticed always happened in the late afternoon. We'd hear the crunch of car tires pulling around the circular drive to the back of the house. That sound would stop, and then we would hear a car door open and close. In the beginning, we would hurry outside, thinking we had guests. We would find the driveway empty. We'd look across at our neighbors' driveways, but there would be nothing there to account for what we had heard.

Shortly after the sounds in the driveway started, we began to feel a "presence" in the master bedroom, just off the garage. We felt something watching us as we read, talked, or did any of our normal daily activities. Even though we didn't tell anyone outside our family, we believed our visitors felt it, too. It was especially evident when our guests sat on the couch near the hall door that led back to that master bedroom. They would start to fidget and glance over their shoulders. Some would get up and move to another seat in the living room away from the door.

Often they would ask, "Is there someone in your back bedroom?"

We'd say, "No. Why do you ask?"

Usually they would reply, "I don't know. I just felt like someone was watching me."

We soon realized that the only way we could get any relief from our invisible watcher was to leave a light on in what we came to call "our haunted bedroom."

Knowing we had a ghost, we set about to learn all we could about the house itself. First, we discovered a spot of cold air inside the bedroom near the door that led to the hall. We checked it at various times, but the cold spot never changed, regardless of the changes in temperature around it. If we turned on the heat or the air conditioning, or if we opened or closed the windows, the cold spot remained the same.

We tried to learn the history of the house, but official records gave us little information. The house had been moved from another location during World War II and had been remodeled. No other records were available.

Once, while we were playing with the Ouija board (something I no longer recommend doing), we asked it to tell us about the house. The Ouija board was just a game to us then. We never dreamed that it might be a way of contacting spirits we didn't want. We asked it to tell us about the house.

The pointer on the board spelled out several bits of information. It told us that a previous owner was a man named Ray. It said there was a small wall compartment in the haunted bedroom that would confirm that it was telling the truth. The rest of the messages were too garbled to verify, but the board mentioned a mother, her son, and someone her son had killed in the house. We didn't feel particularly enlightened by the Ouija board, and we never thought about it again until Ervin knocked out part of the bedroom wall to enlarge the closet.

"Come here quick and look at this!" he called.

Fatima and I ran to the door and looked toward the wall where Ervin was pointing. We couldn't believe it. There in the wall was a small compartment that might have once held a wall safe. On a tiny scrap of yellowed paper stuck between the two-by-fours was the word *Ray*. It was weird, but it was another dead end. Without a last name, we couldn't look for records.

Ghostly things began to happen in quick succession after that. Twice while we were eating lunch, we heard sounds like rocks or bricks hitting the side of the house. That was followed by sounds of garbage being dumped. We ran outside, but nothing was disturbed.

One night after Ervin left to work the second shift, my sister, my nephew, and I heard on the news that severe thunderstorms were predicted before morning. My nephew's dog, Inky, was a good guard dog, but she was terrified of storms. Before we went to bed that night, we brought her into the garage so she'd feel safe.

About midnight, a terrible pounding on the side of the garage woke us. It was much too loud to be made by a person. We jumped out of bed, thinking a violent storm had hit. To our amazement, when we looked out we saw that it was not storming at all. The deafening banging continued, but we did not hear Inky barking any warning of intruders. We opened the inside garage door to check on her and found her huddled, trembling, as close to the inside door as she could get. She was staring at the wall where the pounding was centered, too terrified to move. There was no window in the wall, so we couldn't see what was out there without going outside, and we weren't about to do that.

The pounding finally stopped, but we were still too scared to go out to see if anything was there. We were sure that whatever had been hitting the house with such force must have caused some damage. We brought Inky inside with us and waited for Ervin to come home.

As soon as he pulled into the garage, we rushed out to relate what had happened. He went out and checked the wall, but he couldn't find a scratch on anything.

Ervin was inclined at first to think that we were just afraid to be alone at night while he was at work. Then he experienced some strange occurrences that convinced him that we were not imagining things.

My nephew went away to summer band camp for a week, and Fatima and I decided to take a short trip to visit some relatives for the weekend. Ervin stayed home alone because he had to work. He worked at night and slept during the day, so he went to bed as soon as we left, expecting to get a good rest. Instead, he began to hear footsteps walking in the living room. He sat up in bed to make sure he was awake. The footsteps still clicked clearly on the hardwood floor. He got up to see if we had come back. As he entered the living room, he was almost overcome by the smell of strong perfume that he knew we didn't wear. Nobody was in the room. He checked all the doors and windows; all were securely locked.

After this experience, we noticed that objects in the house began to appear and disappear mysteriously. A ring that was kept in one jewelry box turned up in another one. An old watch that didn't belong to any of us showed up in a box one day with other jewelry. The watch kept perfect time until 2:00 A.M. every day, and then it stopped. Ervin took it to a jeweler and had it checked thoroughly, but the jeweler found nothing wrong. One day Fatima opened the closet and found an old pair of shoes that had not been there before. We asked everyone who had been to the house if the shoes were theirs, but nobody owned them. It was another mystery we never solved.

One day Fatima and I cleaned the haunted room and looked back as we stepped out into the hall. We saw something sticking out from under the bed that hadn't been there when we had just cleaned. Nobody could have sneaked in and put it in there because the two of us were alone in the house with the doors locked. We pulled the object out from under the bed and saw that it was an old red-checked tablecloth that wasn't ours. Nobody ever claimed it.

Another strange thing happened one sunny afternoon when Fatima was walking across the front yard from the mailbox. She looked up and saw an old handmade chair on the front porch. We never left chairs on the front porch, so Fatima hurried toward it to check it out. As she got near, it simply vanished.

Once when Ervin was mowing, Fatima stayed inside to wash the dishes. She had almost finished when she glimpsed a movement in the hall that led from the haunted bedroom to the living room. She saw a man's back as he went from the hall into the living room. It was a terribly hot day, so she assumed it was Ervin taking a break from mowing.

"Did it get too hot for you?" she called out.

There was no answer. She became alarmed, thinking maybe Ervin might be sick from too much sun. She hurried to the living room, expecting to see him passed out, but the room was empty. She checked the front door, but it was still locked from the inside. Nobody could have gone out that way. She looked out the window and saw Ervin mowing at the edge of the backyard.

The only other person to see a ghostly figure in the house was Ervin's mother, Katie. She came for a visit once while I was staying there for the summer. We told her nothing about the eerie experiences in the house, so she had no reason to expect anything strange to disturb her when she chose to sleep in the haunted bedroom. She was tired from her trip, so she went to bed early to get a good night's rest. When she came to breakfast the next morning, she looked anything but rested.

"Who was that man who came into my room last night after I went to bed?" she demanded to know.

"Nobody was in your room, Mom," Ervin told her.

"Yes, there was," she said. "I saw him!"

"We'd never let someone just walk into your room," Fatima assured her. "Maybe you were dreaming."

"I wasn't dreaming!" Katie insisted. "Some man was in there. I woke up sometime before daylight and saw him standing at the foot of my bed, looking at me. It scared me half to death! I thought he was a burglar."

"What did you do?" I asked.

"I asked him what he was doing in my room," she said. "I sat up in bed, and he disappeared. I know I wasn't dreaming, though."

We all tried to put Katie's experience out of our minds and enjoy her visit. A few days later, she was looking through a picture album when she gasped and pointed to a picture.

"That's him!" she said. "That's the man who was in my room the other night."

Fatima and Ervin looked at the picture. It was a friend of theirs who had been in their home many times, but Katie had never met him. He had died in a plane crash a year before her visit.

After Katie went home, we had a few uneventful days. Then one hot, sticky, humid summer afternoon, our neighbors and Fatima and I were lured outside with our lawn chairs by a cool, refreshing breeze that had begun to blow unexpectedly. Dogs lay in yards enjoying the relief, and garage doors were left open so the garages could air out. It was a picture-book scene of serenity. Fatima and I had just settled down with books to read when a terrible commotion began up the street. The dogs in the yards along the block jumped up, bristling and barking and baring their teeth. We, along with our neighbors, all turned in that direction to see what was causing the disturbance. We were puzzled when we saw nothing but the dogs. They were snarling and jumping at something none of us could see. The dogs became quiet when the unseen intruder passed them, and watched as the dogs in the next yard took up the protest. The neighbor next door scolded his dogs, but they ignored him and continued to lunge at the invisible trespasser.

Yard by yard, the thing we couldn't see came closer. The cool breeze turned cold, and we shivered. When the trespasser got to us, my nephew's dogs, Tuff and Inky, looked toward our open garage and barked viciously. Time seemed suspended.

Then, whatever it was evidently turned and retraced its steps. Tuff and Inky turned their heads as if watching it come out of our garage and start back up the block. They howled and barked until the other dogs took up the barking as the unseen thing returned the way it had come. Neighbors talked about it for days, but nobody could explain it.

Something else that defied logic took place inside that house. My nephew's girlfriend asked my sister to bake her a birthday cake. Fatima was happy to do it. She baked it early in the morning so it would have time to cool before she put the icing on it. When she took the cake from the oven, she carefully placed it on the table in the little breakfast nook. It smelled so good that Ervin and I went in for a closer look. The three of us stood there thinking how good it was going to taste later with the icing. Suddenly, right before our eyes, the cake started coming apart in perfect pieces. It was not crumbling! It looked like someone was cutting it with an invisible knife. We never told the girl that a ghostly helper had joined her birthday celebration.

Ervin eventually got another job, and he and his family moved away. The next summer, we drove by and saw a "For Sale" sign in front of their old house. We knew the house wasn't really empty, though. That house will probably always be occupied by residents that are not of this world.

The Haunted Mansion

LB: In August 1998, Roberta and I were invited to tour a supposedly haunted mansion near the Ohio River. The owners have requested anonymity, and I will honor that request.

Dark clouds rolled in as we arrived, adding a spooky atmosphere for our visit. Our host and hostess greeted us at the door and ushered us inside before the rain began. My interest in the old house was not to search out spooks, as Roberta hoped to do. The historic building itself, with its high ceilings, arched windows, marble fireplaces, and carved rosewood staircase, fascinated me.

Our host told us that the house had originally been

built by a man who gave it to his wife as a wedding present. They both died of natural causes in the house many years later. Through the years, the ghost of the wife had been seen many times in the house near her bedroom on the second floor where she died. The current owners had made many renovations after they bought the place. They joked that maybe the ghost stayed around to make sure that they did things right.

While our hostess made refreshments for us downstairs, her husband took us on a tour. He went up the stairs first, Roberta followed, and I walked close behind her. We had almost reached the second-floor landing beside the room where the lady had died when I heard soft footsteps coming up the steps behind me. I felt a presence draw very near. It felt so real that I thought it was someone trying to pass us. I assumed it was our hostess coming to join us. I reached out and touched Roberta's shoulder.

"Move over, Hon," I told her. "The lady wants to get by."

We all stopped and turned around, but nobody was on the stairs. We all felt a sudden chill, but the presence never materialized. It disappeared as quickly as it came, leaving behind the faint scent of a woman's perfume.

We finished our tour, had refreshments, and left just as the rain ended. As we started to step out the door, loud thumps came from the bedroom at the top of the stairs. Since the four of us were together by the door, the noise had to be made from something other than us. We figured it was the ghost's way of saying good-bye.

River Ghost

LB: A couple named Ramsey lived in a big old farmhouse in a little river town in Kentucky. Mr. Ramsey was said to be a mean old cuss who beat his wife on a regular basis. People walking past on the river road could hear her moans and groans if the beatings were in progress or if they passed by shortly after he had finished. Sometimes on warm summer evenings they would see her walking by the river, staring at the water and crying.

That's just the way things were back then. Neighbors minded their own business when it came to what went on between a husband and his wife. Mrs. Ramsey took the beatings because she had no place to go and no skills to go off on her own to work and earn a living.

Shortly before he died, Mr. Ramsey willed all of his property to his nephew. It must have been one of his better days, because he made a provision in his will for his wife to live on the land until her death.

After Mr. Ramsey died, his nephew proved to be made from the same mean mold as his uncle. He couldn't legally turn Mrs. Ramsey out of the house, but he could—and did—go there and make life miserable for her. He was especially mean if he needed money for whiskey. He would carry out her possessions to sell and fling her across the room if she tried to stop him.

"Hurry and die, old woman!" he would sneer at her. "Then this house will be all mine!"

"You will never enjoy this property when I am gone," she declared. "I will never leave this house, no matter what you say!"

Maybe the nephew got tired of waiting and took matters into his own hands. Or maybe Mrs. Ramsey really did slip on the muddy riverbank one summer morning and drown in the river. Was her death an accident, or was she pushed? Nobody saw it happen, so her death was declared an accident.

The nephew took possession of the house and moved in with his family before Mrs. Ramsey was hardly cold in her grave. He thought he was now set for life. Mrs. Ramsey's vow never to leave the house was forgotten—until the family went to sleep that first night.

The man's children woke him at midnight, screaming. He and his wife ran to their room to see what was wrong. Mrs. Ramsey's ghostly form floated near the ceiling, and she silently pointed a finger at him when he came into the room.

"Get out!" he screamed at her, and he threw a shoe at the ceiling.

The ghost vanished, and the family went back to bed. They were quite shaken, but they finally went back to sleep. Then the sound of loud moans and groans woke him.

"Get out!" he shouted. "This is my house!"

To his surprise, the noise ceased for the rest of the night. The nephew and his family were not to find peace in the house, though. Every night, moans and groans and sometimes footsteps would wake the entire family. The lack of sleep began to take its toll. They didn't know how much longer they could stand it. The nephew was a stubborn man, though, and he was determined to outlast the old woman's ghost and live on his land.

Then, one hot night late in summer a storm approached, with thunder so loud that it drowned out the ghostly sounds. The wind hit with such force that the whole house shook. A lightning bolt streaked across the sky and struck the roof, engulfing it with fierce flames that ate their way to the foundation in minutes. The nephew and his family were lucky to escape with their lives.

The nephew sold the land to a neighbor, who used it only for crops, and never set foot there again. The old foundation remained by the river for many years. Neighbors walking by on summer nights could sometimes hear Mrs. Ramsey moaning and groaning like she used to. A few saw her walking by the river, staring at the water, crying as she did when she was alive. Nobody ever lingered or tried to speak to her. They hurried on their way and silently wished her well.

Fred's Ghost

RB: My sister Fatima told me this story of a strange dream.

I grew up with Fred and his two younger brothers, Carl and Clyde. They had no sisters and I had no brothers, so we were like family. Their family's farm joined ours, so we saw each other almost every day. They walked me to school, church, and almost every other event in our small Kentucky community. They were my big brothers, my protectors who always made everything right.

One weekend Fred went on a trip to Tennessee with some friends. As they were driving back home, they were involved in a head-on collision. Fred was killed instantly. Just like that, he was gone from my life. I couldn't believe it. I had lost part of myself in that fatal accident.

It wasn't the same for any of us without Fred. We looked to see his smiling face as he came through the door. We listened for his voice, but he was not there. I married and moved away. Carl, Fred's middle brother, joined the U.S. Marines. Clyde, his youngest brother, joined the Army and was sent to Korea. We all wrote to each other quite often, and we all wrote to Fred's mother, Anna, too.

When summer came, Clyde's letters stopped coming. We all contacted each other, but nobody, not even his mother, had heard from him. The fighting was heavy in Korea then, and we all feared the worst. Anna was beside herself with worry. Death had taken her husband and her son Fred. She couldn't face losing another son so soon. We didn't know how to comfort her.

Then, while spending the weekend on the farm with Mom and Dad, I had a dream I'll never forget. I saw Fred coming down the road toward the house, just as he used to do when we were teenagers. He walked to the edge of the yard, but stopped just outside the light from the window.

"Hey!" I called to him.

"Hey!" he answered.

"Come on in!" I invited.

"I can't come into the light," he said, "but I have something to tell you about Clyde. He's wounded, but he's in a hospital. He'll be all right. Tell Mom she will hear in a few more days."

Then the darkness closed in around him and he was gone. I woke up and felt his presence so strongly that I was afraid to get up.

The next day, I immediately went to visit Anna. I told her my dream. She said it was a comfort to her.

In few days, she received a letter from Clyde. It was exactly as Fred had told me it would be. Clyde was wounded and would soon be sent to the United States to recover.

It was a comfort to me to think of Fred's visit, even if it was in a dream. My "big brother" was still around to tell me that everything would be all right.

Mist on Cane Run

LB: One night in the summer I went riding with some friends along Cane Run Road in Louisville. The young man who was driving was proud of his new car, so we had all looked at every inch of it before we started out.

As we approached a narrow bridge, a white, misty figure rose up from beside the bridge and tried to get in the car through the windshield. We could hear it scratching on the metal roof, trying to get inside. Frightened, the young man sped away, and we lost the misty figure.

We were all a little shaken, so we pulled over as soon as we could to get our wits about us.

"What on earth was that?" someone asked.

"Could that just have been fog?" the driver asked.

We didn't think so, but we hoped that was all it had been. We got out and checked the car. It was scratched where the thing had been, and we knew the scratches hadn't been there before.

Later in the summer, I went riding down Cane Run Road with my uncle. We were near the same bridge when out of nowhere came a greenish-blue mist in front of us. It turned into the shape of a woman, standing in the middle of the road and looking as though she was screaming for help. My uncle hit the brakes and skidded sideways, but we couldn't stop; the car went right through the figure. I looked back, and there was nothing there at all. My uncle stopped the car and we both went back to where we had seen the figure, but there was no sign of anyone.

Afterward, my uncle asked around and learned that a woman had died in an accident at that spot several years ago when her car hit the bridge. Could her ghost still be there?

For a long time, our car would act up every time we went down Cane Run Road. The lights would blink on and off, and the front end would shimmy. It only happened at that one spot.

I haven't been by the bridge in a long time. Maybe the poor ghost eventually got somebody to help her pass on to the other side.

Unwanted Tenants

RB: Roy Hayes moved his wife, Joann, and their small son when he was working on a construction project in northern Kentucky one summer. They were delighted to rent a nice old house for a very reasonable amount of money.

Roy went to work and left his wife to unpack. Just after he had gone, Joann was in the kitchen putting dishes in the cabinet when she heard a loud noise in the hallway. Thinking it was the baby, who was just big enough to crawl and pull up on things, she raced out to the hall to see if maybe he had turned a box over. She was right about the box, but not the baby. In the hall, she discovered that a huge box of household items had been dumped on the floor, but she could see the baby sleeping on a quilt in the living room where she had put him down for a nap!

As that day progressed and others followed, strange things continued to happen. The chandelier in the dining room would swing at Joann every time she passed. Often while she cooked, something furry would brush against her leg, but they had no pets. She tried to ignore these things, but eventually they so upset her that she finally told her husband.

Roy didn't believe Joann at first. He insisted that she get a complete physical examination, but the doctor found nothing wrong. Because Joann was clearly upset by the house, the doctor suggested that they move. It wasn't easy to find a place just for the summer, however, especially at such a low cost, so they decided to stay where they were until the construction project was over.

Roy didn't want to leave Joann and the baby alone, so a neighbor offered to stay with her while Roy was at work. Nothing happened while the neighbor was there, so after a time everyone began to breathe easier. Roy believed that the problem was in Joann's mind—until he began to have the same experiences. The chandelier swung at him one day, and another day when he was wearing shorts he felt a furry thing rub against his leg in the kitchen.

Things started to get worse. One morning, Roy found his toothbrush sticking in a tiny crack in the high ceiling of the bathroom. Every morning, he found a little red tricycle in the driveway outside the garage. There were no children in the neighborhood old enough to ride a tricycle.

Roy and some of his construction-worker buddies decided to make a complete search of the house and the garage. The garage was empty except for a couple of rusty tools. They found nothing wrong with the chandelier. Then they turned their attention to the attic.

In the front of the attic, they found a small room that had been boarded up. They broke in and found bars on the window. They found a rusty red tricycle, some old quilts on the floor, and a rag doll. They wondered if a child had been held captive in that attic room.

Soon after the discovery of the room, some unseen presence began throwing furniture all around the house. At that point Roy and Joann gave up the idea of staying until the construction project was over. They found a small house at a higher price in another part of town and packed to leave.

Friends helped them on moving day. As they carried out the last load, a muffled laugh sounded from upstairs. They all looked up and saw the apparition of a man and a small child standing at the window, watching the unwanted tenants go.

When a Voice Calls, Don't Answer

RB: My sister Fatima had this experience and shared it with me.

My husband and I hadn't been married very long when we moved to a small community outside of Harrodsburg, Kentucky. I was delighted to find that a young couple, Kezzie and Jimmy Smith, lived next door. Kezzie and I became good friends and kept each other company while our husbands worked.

One summer afternoon, Kezzie offered to give me a home permanent. The permanent lotion did not smell very good, so we moved to the back porch so we wouldn't stink up Kezzie's house. She finished the last application of lotion and looked at the clock so she could time the permanent. It was exactly noon.

Suddenly, we heard a voice frantically calling, "Mrs. Smith! Mrs. Smith! Mrs. Smith!"

It was coming from the front of the house, so we ran to see what was wrong. To our surprise, nobody was there.

Puzzled, we went back to the porch to finish the perm. As soon as we sat down, the voice called again.

"Mrs. Smith! Mrs. Smith! Mrs. Smith!"

Again we rushed to the front and searched all around the house, but we found nothing.

We went back to rinse my hair and apply the neutralizer, but the frantic voice sounded a third time.

"Mrs. Smith! Mrs. Smith! Mrs. Smith!"

"If somebody is playing a joke, let's catch them," whispered Kezzie. "You go around the house that way and I'll go this way."

We circled the house, but we found no one.

Later that day, Kezzie's mother came to visit. Kezzie told her about our strange experience. Her mom looked concerned.

"You didn't answer the voice, did you?" she asked.

"Yes," said Kezzie. "We went looking for it."

"You shouldn't have," her mom said. "If you answer a voice that calls you three times, it means somebody is going to die very soon."

Kezzie laughed it off, but I was worried. I had heard that old superstition many times, and I knew that sometimes it proved to be true.

The next day Kezzie asked me over for lunch. She wanted to see how the perm had turned out. It was a little after noon when we started to eat. We heard a car stop out front and then we heard a knock at the door.

"Mrs. Smith!" a voice called.

We looked at each other, thinking *Not again!*

We went to the door, and there stood the sheriff.

"Mrs. Smith," he began, his voice choking a bit. "Mrs.

Smith, I am sorry to have to bring you some bad news. Your husband, Jimmy, has just had an accident down the road. He died at the scene."

Both of us remembered the voice from the day before. It came at the same time as Jimmy's death.

Music Parties

LB: In the old days, summer entertainment on Saturday nights often consisted of music parties at various homes. Neighbors would gather at the designated place and play music and dance the night away. The best fiddler was Marshall Frost, so his house was a favorite. Besides, his wife made cookies that would melt in your mouth, and she served them with cold milk that had been stored in the spring.

John Burton was one neighbor who did not join in. He thought fiddle playing and dancing were sinful. His daughter Emily was always pestering him to let her go to one of the parties, but he refused.

"I forbid you to set foot in such a place," he told her. "Such carrying on is disgraceful."

Emily could hear the music and the laughter from her room at night and she longed to be a part of the fun. One night, after her father had gone to sleep, she decided to sneak out and see for herself what the parties were like. She told herself she wouldn't stay but a few minutes.

After Emily got to the Frosts' house, she stood on the sidelines, watching the dancing and tapping her foot to the music. One song followed another, and she lost all track of time. When Marshall Frost's wife brought out the milk and cookies, Emily accepted with a smile.

She had just bitten off a big chunk of cookie when she saw her father coming toward her, scowling. Startled, Emily gasped, and her quick intake of breath caused the bite of cookie to lodge in her throat. She grabbed her throat and coughed, but the cookie did not budge.

People around her saw what was happening and tried to help by thumping her on the back. The cookie remained lodged. Her father, more frightened now than angry, shook her in an attempt to jar the cookie loose, but it did no good. The horrified bystanders watched as the girl struggled for breath and fell to the ground, dead. It was unbelievable—one minute she was fine, and the next she was gone. Attempts to revive her failed, and finally John Burton picked up the body of his daughter and carried her home. The tragedy sent the others home, too.

After the funeral, Marshall Frost and the neighbors did not have a music party for three weeks. When they resumed their partying the following Saturday, John Burton heard the music and was instantly enraged.

Grabbing his gun, he ran to Marshall's house as fast as he could go.

"My daughter is dead, and you dare disrespect her by playing music and dancing!" he bellowed.

"John, I'm sorry about your daughter," Marshall said, "but her death was a terrible accident. My fiddling didn't have a thing to do with it."

"It's your fault she was here," John said to Marshall. "I will not let you play that fiddle!"

"This is my property, John," said Marshall. "I will play my fiddle all I want. You had better go on home now."

John clutched his gun. Slowly, he raised it, pointed it at Marshall, and pulled the trigger. Marshall fell dead at John's feet. Then John turned the gun on himself.

Years have passed, and music parties are pretty much a thing of the past. But if you are ever passing by Marshall Frost's old farm, you may hear him playing his fiddle when he wants to, just like he said he would. But beware! The sound of shots will ring out to let you know that the ghost of John Burton still lurks about. Emily's father is still angry about the music.

Mystery Tenants

LB: It was early June when Mr. Willis decided to rent the small cabin on his farm to a couple named Brooks. A construction company was employing Mr. Brooks for the summer, and he told Mr. Willis that the cabin would be fine for him and his wife.

The couple moved in. They kept to themselves. Neighbors soon started talking about Mr. Brooks's loud voice coming from the cabin at night as soon as he came home from work. It seemed that he was fighting with his wife, but her voice was seldom heard. She could be heard moaning, though, so neighbors figured Brooks was probably a wife beater.

Although Mr. Brooks was seen leaving for work every morning, Mrs. Brooks was seldom seen at all. This caused curiosity among the neighbors, especially Mrs. Edmonds, who lived on the farm across the road.

One morning, after Mr. Brooks had left for work, Mrs. Edmonds said to her husband, "I am going over and invite Mrs. Brooks to church Sunday. I want to see if I can find out what is going on over there."

Mr. Edmonds just shook his head as his wife crossed the road to the cabin.

At first Mrs. Edmonds thought that nobody was going to answer her knocks, but then Mrs. Brooks opened the door. Mrs. Edmonds introduced herself, but Mrs. Brooks did not invite her in.

"I was lying down," she said. "I am not feeling well today."

"I'm sorry," said Mrs. Edmonds. "Is there anything I can do?"

"No thanks," said Mrs. Brooks. "I'll be all right."

She started to close the door, but Mrs. Edmonds continued, "I came by to invite you and your husband to church Sunday. There's all-day preaching and dinner on the grounds. You could meet all your neighbors."

"I'll talk to my husband about it," Mrs. Brooks answered, and she closed the door before Mrs. Edmonds could say another word.

"Humph!" Mrs. Edmonds muttered to herself. "No wonder she's sick! It's too hot to keep that door closed."

The Brookses did not show up for church Sunday, and Mr. Edmonds persuaded his wife to let the matter drop. It was really none of their business.

Things had been quiet at the Brooks place for a few days after Mrs. Edmonds's visit, but soon the fighting started again. Mrs. Edmonds heard Mrs. Brooks this time, too, but she couldn't make out what she was saying. After that, nobody saw Mrs. Brooks at all.

A couple of days after she had last heard his wife, Mrs. Edmonds was outside watering her flowers when she noticed Mr. Brooks leaving for work. She asked him how Mrs. Brooks was feeling.

"She's fine," he said. "She's gone to visit her sister."

As he hurried off, Mrs. Edmonds wondered if maybe Mrs. Brooks had left her husband because of the abuse. She hoped that was the case.

For the next three days, Mrs. Edmonds saw neither Mr. nor Mrs. Brooks leave the cabin. Finally she called the landlord, Mr. Willis, and told him about the strange absences. Mr. Willis said the Brookses' rent was due, so he'd go by and collect it and check on the couple.

When the landlord arrived, to his amazement, he found that nobody was there. What's more, the cabin was empty, completely cleaned out!

Mr. Willis didn't hear from Mr. or Mrs. Brooks for some time, so he rented the house to another couple. The new tenant asked if his wife could store some of her canned goods in the old storm cellar out back.

"I don't mind," said Mr. Willis, "but let's see what condition it's in. Nobody's used it for years."

The two men opened the cellar door, and a musty, rotting odor sent them reeling back a few steps.

"Some animal must have gotten trapped and died in there," remarked the new tenant.

The two men breathed deeply and braced themselves against the foul smell as they descended the steps into the cellar. They saw no animal, but the dirt of the cellar floor had been disturbed.

"I hope this is not what I think it is," Mr. Willis said. "Come on. We'd better call the sheriff."

When the sheriff arrived and checked the disturbed area, he found a woman's body, badly decomposed. A close examination revealed that it was Mrs. Brooks. The sheriff looked for Mr. Brooks, but he was never found.

The new tenants stayed on in the cabin, but at night they would often be awakened by the sound of moaning and a bad smell coming from that cellar. They never went down there, even when bad storms came through. Needless to say, they found another place to store their canned food.

Ghost Chains

RB: There's a house on a hill in south central Kentucky that is said to be haunted. People say that nobody has lived in that house for more than two days in the past twenty-five years.

About twenty-five years ago, a man who lived there became very depressed about a money problem he had. He had taken out a loan on the place, and now he couldn't pay it off. He thought he was going to lose his house and farm.

"I've put my blood, sweat, and tears into this place," he told his wife. "I can't stand to see somebody else have it."

His wife tried to console him.

"We can sell off some of the timber and you can hire out and make some extra money," she said. "I can take in sewing."

Her husband wouldn't allow himself to be convinced. He waited until he was alone in the house and then the poor man hanged himself with a logging chain. He put that chain around his neck, threw the chain over the stair railing on the second floor, and jumped off. The chain cut his throat and the blood formed a puddle by the stairs in the hall where he was hanging.

It was a hot summer day, and his wife had gone over to visit a neighbor. When she got home, she opened the screen door and heard something in the hall.

Drip! Drip! Drip!

She walked into the hall and found her husband hanging there. The neighbors heard her screaming and ran over. They called the doctor and the sheriff, and they put the distraught woman to bed. After they came and took the body away, she got up and scrubbed the floor until all the blood was gone.

After the funeral, she went back home. She opened the door and heard something again.

Drip! Drip! Drip!

She walked into the hall and saw that the blood was back!

I was too upset to clean it all up before, she thought to herself.

She scrubbed the floor again and went to bed. Before she could fall asleep, however, she heard footsteps and the sound of a chain being dragged down the hall. She got up to look, but nobody was there. Then she heard that sound again:

Drip! Drip! Drip!

She went to the hall and saw that the blood was back again, just like before. This time, she could not reason with herself.

I cleaned it all up, she thought. *I know I did! But now it's back! He's back! But he can't be! He's dead!*

She screamed so loudly that her neighbors heard her again. They called the sheriff and went over to see what was wrong. The woman was sitting on the steps, staring at the blood.

Her eyes were fixed, and she was unresponsive. She had gone stark, raving mad. The neighbors took the woman away, but she died a few months later in a mental institution.

Her brother paid off the loan and moved his family into the farmhouse. Before they went to bed the first night, they put a thick rug over the place where the blood had been. They were dozing off when the rattle of a chain woke them. Then they heard footsteps and a crashing sound.

They ran to see what was going on. They saw nothing out of place, but they did hear another sound.

Drip! Drip! Drip!

They checked the rug in the hall. It was covered in blood. That was more than enough for them. They packed their belongings and were completely moved out in two days.

Through the years, the brother tried to rent out the place. People would move in, but nobody would stay. The dragging chain, the dripping blood, and the footsteps were too much for even the bravest souls.

He finally sold it to a young couple who said they didn't believe in such things as haunted houses. They replaced the boards in the hall and settled in.

The first night made believers out of them. Footsteps woke them. The chain rattled. The blood dripped. The young couple fled and came back for their things in the light of day.

After that, the old house was abandoned. At night, even now, when people get near the place on hot summer nights, they can hear the footsteps and the chain. Nobody seems to want to go inside, though, to see if the blood is still there, *dripping, dripping, dripping!*

When the Clock Strikes Twelve

RB: It was corn-hoeing time, and the Kenton family was working hard under the hot summer sun to finish before the threatening storm clouds moved in from the west.

"I'm hungry," said little Will. "Can't we stop and eat?"

Dan Kenton leaned on his hoe and looked at his young

son. Then he looked at the western sky to try to determine what the clouds were going to do. They seemed to be drawing around, going up the river. They probably wouldn't get any rain from them, so it seemed safe to take a break. Besides, he was hungry, too.

"Okay," Dan said to his son. "It's almost noon. Let's eat and then go back to work."

They went back to the house and took out some beans and cornbread left over from the night before. They sat down and ate as quickly as they could. At noon, the clock on the mantel began to strike the hour, but it didn't stop at twelve. To their surprise, it kept striking and striking until Dan finally got up and stopped it manually.

The family was puzzled. Dan's mother had given them the clock, and it had always worked perfectly. It had never done anything like that before.

They put the incident out of their minds and went back to the field. They finished hoeing just as another cloud appeared on the horizon. They hurried to the house before the rain set in. They were eating supper when they heard a knock on the door.

"Who would be out in this storm?" Dan asked aloud, as he got up to answer the door. He was surprised to find the sheriff standing there.

"Dan," said the sheriff, "since you don't have a phone, I have to bring you some bad news. Your mother died at noon today."

The family looked at each other, remembering the striking of the clock that went on and on at noon. Had Dan's mother tried to communicate with them at the time of her death?

Dan didn't wind the clock after that. It was beautiful, though, so they left it on the mantel. A year passed, and they forgot about the strange coincidence.

Summer came again. After working in the fields all morning, the family had gathered around the table for their noon meal. Dan wasn't as hungry as usual. His stomach had been hurting all morning. Suddenly the clock started striking. It hadn't been wound, so it couldn't be striking. But it was! It struck twelve and went on striking. Dan started to get up to stop it manually as he had before, but as soon as he was up from the table, he clutched his heart and fell forward. He was dead of a massive heart attack by the time he hit the floor.

"Wonder why the clock struck like that," said little Will after the funeral.

The rest of the family wondered, too, but nobody had the answer. Dan's wife took the clock to a jeweler to be checked. He could find nothing wrong with the clock, and he had no explanation for how an unwound clock would suddenly start striking.

Mrs. Kenton took the clock home and packed it away in the attic. She didn't want to see or think about the strange clock anymore.

Years passed. Dan's widow became old and ill and had to be put in a nursing home. Young Will grew up, married, and moved into the old home place with his wife, Ruby.

One day when Will went off to visit his mother in the nursing home, Ruby decided to look for some dishes her mother-in-law had packed away in the attic. It was noon when she opened the box that contained the clock. As she lifted it from the box for a closer look, the clock began to strike twelve. It struck and struck, and regardless of what she did, it wouldn't stop. Frightened, she threw the clock back into the box and ran from the attic.

Three hours later, Will came home from visiting his mother. Ruby knew something was wrong the minute she saw him.

"What's the matter?" she asked, running to him.

"It's Mom," he told her. "She died in the nursing home at noon today."

Where is the old clock today? They say it was sold at an auction, so it could be anywhere now waiting to strike on and on, warning someone that death is very near.

The Headless Man

LB: My brother-in-law, Ervin Atchley, told me this story, which happened to him.

When I was a boy, I never had any special interest in the supernatural. I certainly wasn't thinking about anything out of the ordinary one Saturday when I climbed in the wagon with Mom and Dad to go into town. It was a typical summer day, and we were headed into town to do the weekly shopping.

Mom and Dad were seated on the wagon seat and I was sitting on the floor of the wagon bed as we started down Sano Road. The sun was shining down on me, and I was thinking about the ice cream cone I was going to buy when we got to the store.

Mom and Dad were talking about the supplies they were going to get and were paying no attention to me. Suddenly, out of the corner of my eye I saw a man walking beside the road. When he first appeared to me, he was just in line with the wagon seat, but then he dropped back a couple of steps and was right beside me. I thought it was odd that Dad didn't stop and offer him a ride. That was the usual thing to do.

I looked up to see if I knew the man. He was wearing a dark suit in spite of the fact that it was a very hot day. I saw his shoes and his suit, and then I saw the strangest thing I'd ever seen. The man had no head! I must have made a sound, but I don't remember it. I just know that Dad pulled up the team and turned around.

"What's the matter?" he asked me.

"That man by the road!" I said.

"What man?" he asked.

"The man was right there!" I said. "He didn't have a head!"

"Aw, son!" Dad said, but he didn't move the wagon.

We both looked, but there was no man there now. Mom and Dad had not seen him, but I can still see him in my mind to this day.

After that, I looked for that man every time we went

down Sano Road, but I never saw him again. When I was older, I heard stories about a man who was decapitated there in an accident. Maybe it was that man I saw by the road that day out looking for his head. I hope he found it and moved on. I don't want to meet up with him again!

The Chivaree

RB: The chivaree (also spelled shivaree) was an old mountain custom of serenading newlyweds on their wedding night. Couples didn't go away on honeymoon trips back then. They usually had their new home ready and moved right in after the wedding. Neighbors would go to the newlyweds' home, beating on pots and pans and blowing whistles or singing and playing instruments, with the idea of keeping them awake. If the groom was a city fellow, they sometimes took it one step further. They would actually kidnap him, take him someplace nearby, and tie or chain him up for a while. Then they would go back and get him, and the bride would have refreshments waiting when they got home. After that, everybody would go home and leave the couple in peace. It was all good-natured fun.

One chivaree turned tragic, however. Maybe it's a good thing that the old custom has died out.

A young couple, John and Hazel, had a June wedding in the little country church that Hazel had attended all her life. John was from a larger town up the river, but he had agreed to move to the house Hazel's family had built for them on their farm. The ceremony went off without a hitch, and, after a wedding feast and best wishes from their friends and family, the couple left for their new home to start their honeymoon.

The neighbors waited until bedtime. Then they gathered pots, pans, and every noisemaker they could find, and piled the noisemakers and themselves on trucks to head to the couple's home for a chivaree. Low thunder rumbled far in the distant west, but they thought the rain would hold off for a while and give them plenty of time to serenade the young couple.

Meanwhile, John was expecting the noisy visitors, but he was nervous. He watched his new bride put out some cookies and make coffee for the visitors to consume later.

"This whole thing is ridiculous!" John said. "What would happen if we refused to open the door?"

"That would hurt their feelings," Hazel told him. "They don't mean any harm. It's just a social custom."

The noisy band of merrymakers arrived, and John opened the door so he and Hazel could listen to the serenade and greet their well-wishers. Two men in the crowd, Arnold and Ray, had been drinking before they joined the others, so their spirits were even higher than the others' spirits.

"Grab him, Ray!" yelled Arnold. "Let's show him some of the countryside!"

Ray joined right in. "Come on, John!" he said. "Let's take a little ride!"

The two men grabbed John and dragged him to their truck. John struggled to get loose. This turn of events did not please him in the least. He had been a good sport about the chivaree up to this point, but this part gave him a bad feeling. He didn't like the looks of the approaching storm. He called out for help, but everybody was laughing and cheering them on.

Nobody thought much about it as the two men drove off with John. They would leave him somewhere for an hour or so, and then bring him home. After they left, Hazel waited for Ray and Arnold to have their fun and bring John home.

Thunder sounded closer as Arnold and Ray, with their captive, came to a little creek. There was a tiny island in the middle of the creek, and the two men had the same idea. They thought it would be funny to leave John on the island for a while.

"We can chain him to that big rock," Ray suggested. "There's a logging chain on the truck."

"Yeah," laughed Arnold. "It will give him a taste of what married life is going to be like! The Old Ball and Chain!"

Everything was funny, as it often is with two men who'd had too much to drink. They paid no attention to the thunder or the approaching clouds. John noticed, though, and he became concerned now for his safety.

"Come on, guys," he said. "You've had your fun. Now get me home before the rain sets in."

"A little rain won't hurt you," laughed Arnold.

"Let me go, you fools!" John ordered. "This is getting out of hand. You can't leave me out here in a storm!"

The two men gripped John's arms more tightly and

dragged him through the water to the little island. They wrapped the chain around him and secured it to a tree beside the big rock. Then they waded back to the bank and hurried to their truck.

"Wait!" yelled John. "Please don't leave me here!"

Ray and Arnold ignored John, and the truck's motor drowned out his voice as they pulled away. They drove about a half mile and pulled the truck over just as the rain started.

"Reckon we should go back and get him?" asked Ray.

"Naw, not yet," said Arnold. "Let's let him get good and soaked first. He'll be as mad as an old wet hen!"

They sat silently as the rain continued with a steady beat. Both men took another drink and dozed off, not realizing that a flash flood was roaring down the creek and covering the island.

John struggled to free himself, but the chain held and rattled as the wall of water rushed over him. He breathed his last breath before Ray and Arnold woke and realized what they had done. By the time they got to the creek, John's lifeless body was floating by the rock, still chained fast to the tree.

Meanwhile, some neighbors had become worried when the storm hit. They went to check on Hazel and to see if Ray and Arnold had returned with John. When they found the three men hadn't returned, they went to look for them. The water was receding as they joined Ray and Arnold on the bank of the flooded creek. They recovered John's body and, with heavy hearts, they carried him home to Hazel.

After John's funeral, Hazel couldn't bear to live in the house that was to have been their home. She brought no charges against Arnold and Ray. She only wanted to leave the tragic place and put the pain behind her. She went to live with an aunt and never came back.

Even though the law did not hold Ray and Arnold accountable, fate did see to it that they were punished. Every time it rained, they claimed they could hear John's voice calling for help. And worst of all, they could hear that log chain rattle during every storm. The two men drank more and more, and one stormy night, their truck ran off the road and overturned in the creek. Trapped inside their truck, both Ray and Arnold drowned.

After that, no newlyweds were ever subjected to a chivaree in that community.

Rain Barrel

RB: My mother, Lillian Simpson, told me this story about an incident she could never explain.

One summer when I was just a young girl, I went to Wayne County to stay a few days with my Uncle Golce and Aunt Cood to help can beans. They had sons, but the boys didn't like to do things like canning. They preferred to work with their father in the fields.

One night after supper, we were all sitting around, listening to a gentle summer rain falling on the roof. It was soothing, not spooky or scary at all. Suddenly, we heard a baby crying outside.

"Who would be out in the rain with a baby?" asked Aunt Cood.

Uncle Golce got up and went to open the door, thinking it was a neighbor or perhaps some traveler who was stranded and looking for help.

When he opened the door, nobody was there, but the crying sounded louder than ever. He walked out on the porch and looked from side to side, but he didn't see anybody.

"Hello!" he called to the darkness. "Anybody out there?"

There was no answer, but the crying continued. We joined him on the porch and listened. It was coming from around the corner of the house now.

"I think it's coming from the rain barrel," said Uncle Golce. "Come on, boys, and help me look."

They could see nothing in the barrel, so they turned it over and emptied the rainwater into Aunt Cood's washtubs, but there was no baby there. They set the barrel back upright.

The crying continued, and now it seemed to be coming from under the rain barrel. They picked up the barrel and moved it over, but the ground beneath had not been disturbed. Uncle Golce got his shovel and dug down a couple of feet. There was no sign of a baby. Suddenly the crying stopped, so we went to bed with the mystery unsolved.

Later Uncle Golce was talking to a neighbor who said a woman and her baby had lived on that farm during the Civil War. The husband had gone off to war and left his wife to tend the crops. Soldiers came through and took over the house, and the woman and baby were never seen after that. Some people believe that she escaped with her baby and went to live with relatives. Most people believe, though, that the soldiers killed both her and the baby and buried them somewhere in the yard.

Was it that poor dead baby we heard crying in the soft summer rain?

Aunt Sarah's Ghost

RB: Back in the summer of 1995, I was hired to do a storytelling program in Somerset, Kentucky. I was pleasantly surprised when several of my cousins from the area came to hear me. I knew they were all in the audience when I started to tell my stories.

I was halfway through my opening story when I spotted my Aunt Sarah standing near the end of the stage, smiling and listening. I had always loved her and enjoyed visiting her and her family at their house in Somerset. Regardless of how many people were around, she always made everyone feel welcome and special. I was delighted that she had come to my program until it hit me: *Aunt Sarah had been dead for several years!*

I looked around the audience and back to her, thinking my eyes were deceiving me, but she was still there.

It must be my cousin Caroline, I thought. *She looks a lot like her mother.*

I knew that Caroline hadn't come with the other cousins, so I figured she had simply arrived late. I made a mental note to talk to her as soon as I finished my session and went on telling my stories. When I finished, she was no longer there.

I immediately went looking for her, but I couldn't find her. I decided she must have joined my other cousins, so I found them. She wasn't with them, however, and they were puzzled when I told them what I had seen.

We decided to go out for something to eat and figured we'd call Caroline to see if she wanted to join us.

We were shocked when a neighbor answered Caroline's phone. There had been a kitchen fire at Caroline's house just before my program started. The neighbor was there while the firefighters finished cleaning up. It couldn't have been Caroline whom I saw at the program near the stage because while I was telling my stories she was at the hospital getting treated for burns on her hand. The figure I saw had to have been Aunt Sarah's ghost!

The Hanged Man

RB: A long time ago on a bright summer day in Kentucky, a man attacked a little girl who was on her way home from a friend's house. He waited in some bushes till she was passing by, then raped and killed her and left her body in the weeds by the side of the road.

Neighbors heard the little girl's screams and ran to help, but they were too late. They saw the man run away and called the sheriff.

The sheriff tracked the man down and caught him. He was still wearing overalls stained with the girl's blood. The sheriff locked the man up while awaiting trial. He confessed, but since he wasn't quite right in the head, most people believed he wouldn't get punished for the crime. An angry mob stormed the jail. They took the man out and hanged him in a tree near the road. He was buried not in sacred ground, but just outside the graveyard fence, in sight of the tree where he was hanged. As the years passed, many local people reported seeing the man by the graveyard, the hanging tree, or the side of the road.

One rainy night, a couple from another state was passing through town, and they had a flat tire near the graveyard. The man got out and started changing the tire, leaving his wife in the car so she could stay dry. The minute he stepped out of the car, he felt very nervous and uncomfortable.

He thought it was just the dark, rainy night spooking him. He didn't think there was anything really out there to be afraid of, but he hurried just the same. He couldn't shake the feeling that something was watching him. He could see his wife inside the car watching anxiously, but he felt something looking at him outside of the car, too. He was relieved when he finished changing the tire and got back in the car with his wife.

"Folks around here are not very friendly, I guess," she said to him.

"Why do you say that?" he asked her. "We don't even know anybody here."

"Well," replied his wife, "that man in overalls stood

right by the road over there and didn't even say hello or offer to help you!"

"I didn't see any man," he told her nervously, as he drove away. "Your eyes must have been playing tricks on you."

"I know what I saw!" she insisted.

A few miles down the road, they came to a motel and checked in for the night. The proprietors were friendly, so the man and woman told what had happened to them down the road. The people at the motel listened quietly and then told the couple the story of the hanged man.

"You probably encountered his ghost," they told the couple. "You were right there near the hanging tree."

The Guardian

RB: One of the hottest days of summer sent little Annie and her grandmother, Lizzie, from the garden to cool off under the shade of an old beech tree in the backyard.

"Are you all right, Granny?" little Annie asked. "Your face is all red."

"I'm a little dizzy," Lizzie answered. "I got too hot, but I'll be okay when I cool off a bit."

"You're not going to die, are you? I wouldn't have anybody to watch out for me or make me rag dolls," said Annie. She had a family of rag dolls that Lizzie had made for her, and they were Annie's favorite toys.

"I will always watch out for you, Annie," her grandmother told her.

"Do people become guardian angels when they die?" Annie asked.

"I don't think that people actually become angels, but I think my spirit will watch over you," said Lizzie.

Thunder boomed suddenly, and Lizzie and Annie saw that a summer storm was approaching.

"Oh! Look at the lightning!" said Annie.

"We'd better get inside," said Lizzie. "You should never be under a tree in a storm. Can you help me up? I still feel a little dizzy."

Annie helped Lizzie inside, and Annie's mother told Lizzie to lie down. It was very unusual for her to be ill. The storm hit, and the family sat anxiously around Lizzie's bed. She slept so soundly that they couldn't wake her up. When the storm ended Annie's father went for the doctor. The doctor examined Lizzie and gave the family bad news. Lizzie had had a stroke and, sadly, would never wake up.

Annie missed her grandmother. Every day she took her dolls outside and played in the shade of the beech tree. She thought of all the good times and all the talks she and Lizzie had had together. She wondered if her grandmother was really watching over her.

One day when Annie had been outside playing, Annie's mother called her for lunch. Annie left her dolls under the beech tree and hurried inside to eat. The family had just finished the meal when a sudden storm blew up.

"My dolls!" Annie cried. "I left them under the tree! They'll get wet!"

Before anybody realized what she was going to do, Annie ran out the door and headed for the tree.

"Annie, come back!" her mother called, but Annie could not hear above the roar of the wind.

She was under the tree now, and she heard a loud crack above her head. The wind had broken a limb from the old tree and it was coming down on her. Suddenly, Annie found herself flying back from the tree as the limb hit the ground right in front of her. Annie's father dashed from the porch and grabbed her up in his arms. He ran inside with her just as the fury of the storm hit.

"How did you jump back like that?" her mother asked. "I thought the limb was going to crush you."

"Something pulled me!" Annie told her. "I felt somebody take hold of me and yank me back. I thought it was you or Daddy!"

"We couldn't get to you in time," her father said.

"Then it was Granny!" said Annie. "She said she would always watch out for me."

Her parents smiled.

"Maybe so," said her mother.

Just then, Annie remembered why she had run out in the wind. She had left her dolls under the tree. They were probably ruined now. She stepped out on the porch to go look at her dolls under the tree, but then she noticed something next to the wall on the porch. There were her dolls, all lined up, all safe and dry! Annie knew then that her granny had kept her word.

Family Cemetery

LB: In the late 1800s in Kentucky, families had their own cemeteries. The Burton family had started theirs when they moved to a farm and cleared some new ground. It was a peaceful place, dotted with stumps, right beside the road. During that year, a couple of older relatives died and were buried in the little cemetery. The family pulled weeds and kept flowers on the graves.

One summer Grandmother Fanny Mae came down with a fever and died. She had been worried that the rest of the family would catch whatever it was that she had, but they didn't get it. She was buried in the cemetery by a stump next to the road. Everybody took her death hard, especially her daughter Kat.

After her mother's funeral, Kat went to spend the night with her grandmother. When morning came, Kat started home early because she had chores to do. She had to walk down the road right by the cemetery.

As she came in sight of it, she saw a woman sitting on a stump with her back to the road. She thought it was one of the family members putting flowers on Fannie Mae's grave, so she hurried over to see who it was. As she approached, the woman turned. Kat's heart nearly stopped when she saw the woman's face. It was her dead mother, Fannie Mae, whom they had just buried.

"How's the family back home?" Fannie Mae asked.

Kat never gave her an answer. She took off running as

fast as her feet could move. She ran inside her house, gasping for breath, and collapsed in a chair. It took Kat ever so long before she could tell them what happened.

Kat was scared every time she had to pass the cemetery after that, but she never saw the ghost of her mother again. Her mother probably didn't want to scare the poor girl like she did before.

Disturbed Dead

RB: Arthur and his wife, Faye, bought a house in July in a new subdivision, and moved in with their five-year-old son, Artie. It was a split-level house with a finished basement where the family planned to spend a lot of time. The bedrooms were on the top level.

The house looked picture perfect, but little Artie became very fearful the minute they moved in. He had enjoyed having his own room before the family moved, so his parents didn't understand why he did not want to be alone in his room in this new house.

"There's a man in my room," he told them.

His parents opened the closet door and looked under the bed to try to reassure Artie that he was alone, but he still insisted someone was in there.

One night company came over, so Arthur and Faye put Artie to bed early. They took their guests to the basement to play a game of pool. They had just started the game when Artie came running down the stairs.

"There's a man in my room!" he said.

"Artie," Arthur patiently explained to his son, "you know we looked everywhere and there is no man in your room."

"Yes, there is," he insisted, "and he looks mad!"

"Come on," Faye said. "I'll check your room and tuck you in."

As they started upstairs, they all heard a loud thump in Artie's room. They ran to the room and opened the door, but nothing was out of place and nobody was there. They put Artie to sleep on the couch until the guests left. Then they all went to bed.

The next morning, Arthur went to work. Faye was vacuuming the hall upstairs. Artie was playing in the basement, so there was nobody upstairs but Faye. As she worked, she saw something move and looked up to see what it was. She was startled to see the transparent outline of a man come from Artie's room and vanish through the wall!

Faye was very upset. She immediately called the builder of the subdivision. At first, he wasn't very sympathetic. Eventually, however, he admitted that there had been a cemetery where the subdivision was located, but he insisted that they had tried to move all the graves.

"What do you mean, you *tried*?" Faye asked.

"The cemetery was very old," the builder explained. "It's possible that some of the graves were unmarked. If that were the case, then we missed some and built the houses over them."

Once Faye was told about the graves, the ghost never appeared again. Perhaps it was disturbed because nobody knew it was there. Now that it had made its presence known, it was finally at peace.

Ghosts by the Creek

LB: Most young boys in Kentucky like to go fishing on hot summer days. There are few things as peaceful as sitting on the shady bank of a creek, waiting for a fish to nibble your bait. One Kentucky stream in Russell County is said to have ghosts that sometimes interrupt the boys who come to fish there.

According to local stories, it seems that back in the early 1900s, a man lived in a house near the creek with his wife, their baby, and their nine-year-old son. The son spent hours fishing from the creek bank while his dad was at work.

One day the man came home from work early and found his wife with another man. His mind just snapped. In a jealous rage, he grabbed his gun and shot his wife, the other man, and the baby. Then he went outside looking for his nine-year-old son.

The boy heard the shots and saw his dad running toward the creek. Frightened, he ran splashing through the water and tried to hide in the bushes by the bank, but the father found him and shot him, too. Then the father turned the gun on himself and took his own life.

Now when young boys go fishing near that spot, they

sometimes hear the scene reenacted. They hear three gunshots and then they hear footsteps running toward the creek. Suddenly there is splashing in the water, followed shortly by two more shots. Then everything gets deathly quiet. The birds stop singing, the insects stop buzzing, and the air gets heavy. It's at that point that smart boys grab their fishing poles and leave the creek to the ghosts.

The Haunting of Porter Prince

RB: A man named Porter Prince lived in the Kentucky Hills in the late 1800s. His family and another family that lived on the hill above Porter's had been feuding for years over some land. The feud had gone on so long that most parties involved had forgotten the details that started the feud, but stubbornness on each side kept it going.

One summer, Porter's family decided to move to another county. Porter's dad took a couple of loads of furniture and belongings to the new place and then came back for the family and the rest of their possessions. They loaded their wagon this last time and hitched a double team to it to pull it over the steep, rough roads.

As they were getting ready to pull out, the son of the feuding family rode up with a message.

"Pa says for you to stop by on your way out," the young man said. "He says he hates to see you leave with hard feelings. He just wants to settle things."

Porter's dad was a little surprised, but he thought it was

the right thing to do. Both sides needed to put the bad blood behind them.

"Tell your dad that we'll stop by in a few minutes," he said, and the young man rode away to deliver the message.

As the wagon approached the neighbor's yard, all looked serene. Porter's dad stopped the wagon, and the family started to get down from the wagon to say a peaceful goodbye. Suddenly shots rang out from behind the woodpile. It was an ambush, and they had driven right into it!

One shot hit Porter's father in the shoulder. He slumped to the floor of the wagon bed.

"Get the gun!" he shouted to Porter. "Under the seat!"

Porter grabbed it.

"Shoot!" his father ordered. "Shoot!"

Porter blasted away just as the young man who had delivered the message earlier stood up. The shot hit the boy's neck and left his head dangling from his shoulders.

The firing ceased as the feuding family ran to their fallen son. Porter's family got back in the wagon, and Porter's mother grabbed the reins and urged the double team at breakneck speed down the narrow, hilly road to safety.

Porter's dad recovered, but Porter never got over what he had done to the young man. Of course, he'd had no choice. The young man would have shot Porter if Porter had not shot him first. Regardless of the fact that it was self-defense, Porter could never get the image of that dangling head out of his mind.

For the rest of his life, Porter could see the ghost of that headless young man after dark. He did all of his traveling during the day. When the sun set, he never ventured beyond his front porch. He always swore that he could see the young man with the dangling head waiting for him in the shadows.

Summer School

RB: Stories persist in several schools in Kentucky about a haunted band room. There are no facts to back up the stories, but since students have passed it on for years, it definitely could have happened.

Summer school had started, and the band director was taking the opportunity to have his students practice as much as possible for an upcoming event. A boy named Scott practiced his trumpet at home whenever he had a free minute.

One day his mother had heard enough. "Can't you practice somewhere else?" she asked him. "You play that thing loud enough to raise the dead!"

"Okay, Mom," he told her. "I'll find another place."

Scott had an idea. He would go to school after classes were over and practice in the band room. But when he arrived, he found that the doors were already locked for the night. He walked around the building until he came to the band room window. He tried it and found it unlocked. It wasn't a huge window, but it was big enough for Scott to get through with his trumpet. It was high from the band room floor, but there were risers where the students sat to practice.

The risers came nearly to the window, so Scott lowered

his trumpet to the top row. There was a space between the risers and the window, so he thought he could ease through the window backwards and step on the top riser where he had placed his trumpet. As he crawled through, he realized he couldn't turn his head far enough to see the risers. He had to guess about the distance. Unfortunately, he misjudged it, and his foot slipped. He fell to the floor, banging his head against the risers. He never regained consciousness.

When Scott did not come home for supper, his parents began to look for him. Nobody thought about looking inside the school, so they didn't find him until they opened the building for summer school the next morning.

Now strange things happen in that band room. Some people passing by the school when it is supposed to be empty say they see a boy with a trumpet looking out that window. Some students practicing in the band room hear thumps and groans coming from behind the risers. Sometimes at night, custodians know that the room is empty and locked, but they hear a trumpet sounding loud enough to raise the dead!

PART III
GHOSTS OF AUTUMN

Waverly
Hills

Autumn brings Halloween and all the fun of dressing in costumes and going trick-or-treating. In the old days, we did not have to worry about encountering human monsters, nor did we have to be concerned about foreign objects or any unhealthy substances in our treats. The scariest things were the hand-carved jack-o'-lanterns from the homegrown pumpkins in our fields. Tricks were rarely played on anybody, but sometimes pranksters pulled a log across the road or, in extreme cases, turned over an outhouse.

The nights of autumn made people tend to think of ghosts more than in spring and summer. Maybe it was because the leaves were dying and the bare tree branches made noise as they brushed against windowpanes. Unseen things rustled in the leaves, and the autumn wind howled and rattled the shutters and windowpanes like something trying to get in. It took little for the chill in the air to chill our blood. Scarecrows watched us through dead eyes, and shocks of fodder in the cornfields were hiding places for the goblins created in our imagination. Scary Halloween stories abounded!

With the harvest done, people gathered together to share stories. Some of the tales were about werewolves under a full moon; others were of restless spirits lured from their graves by a hook moon that barely glowed in an inky sky. Many of these stories went beyond fantasy. Each one in our circle of tellers was touched in some way by something in a world beyond ours. Our autumn stories were not intended to promote pagan celebrations. Instead, by sharing these experiences, we validated our own sanity and reassured ourselves that there is life beyond the grave.

The Portal Well

RB: The Purvis family had no inkling that anything was wrong with the house on Central Avenue near Churchill Downs when they first moved in. The only odd thing they noticed right away was that the house had two kitchens, and that the plumbing in one of the kitchens was constantly clogged. They called in professional plumbers, but they could not clear up the problem. Since the plumbing in the other kitchen was fine, they looked no further for the cause.

Then one October night, with her husband and two older children away visiting relatives until the next day, Mrs. Purvis and her six-year-old daughter had a very unsettling experience. They had never been afraid before in the house, but since they were alone that night, they decided to sleep together.

It was about one o'clock when a noise in the clogged kitchen woke them. Mrs. Purvis knew she had locked the doors and windows, so she couldn't imagine what was down there. She was hoping it was the clogged pipes making a noise, but then they heard footsteps start. They were absolutely terrified! They lay there, barely breathing, as the footsteps came out of the kitchen into the hall. The mother and daughter held each other and prayed for God to help them as the footsteps moved through the bathroom, the den, the living room, and finally to their bedroom door.

Suddenly, the lights in their bedroom came on, and a cold breeze swept through the room, even though the windows were closed. They saw nothing, but they felt an evil presence in the room with them. They clung to each other, paralyzed with fear, as they watched things happening all around them.

The bottom dresser drawer slowly opened, and from it rose the deflated Christmas reindeer Mrs. Purvis had placed there because her children were fighting over it. It inflated, floated over the foot of the bed, and remained suspended. They could still feel the cold breeze. Mrs. Purvis screamed God's name and the breeze stopped. The reindeer, still inflated, dropped on the foot of the bed. She kicked it off and later got rid of it.

What was the evil presence in the room? Did it appear because the woman and child were alone? Did it choose October to appear because of Halloween? Mrs. Purvis had her own idea of what happened.

She had always believed that there are demonic influences in the world. She had always heard that a demon needs a portal of entry to walk the earth. Since the footsteps began in the clogged kitchen, she decided to check beneath it. When she crawled under there, she discovered a large hole. She immediately called the former owners, and they said the hole was an opening to a deep well. Mrs. Purvis believed that well was the portal where the demon entered.

The family moved not too long after the incident. The house was still there the last time they drove by. Perhaps the well is still there, too. Nobody knows how deep the well is or what was in it or under it. Nobody knows if demons still come through that portal.

Man in the Road

LB: It was a cool Sunday morning in autumn in Russell County. Dad and I had walked across the road from our house and were talking to a neighbor at the edge of his cornfield. Most of the corn had been cut and bundled into fodder shocks for the cattle. Orange pumpkins dotted the field here and there.

As Dad, our neighbor, and I were talking about the crops, we saw a stranger wearing a gray suit coming up the hill toward us. The man, who looked to be about forty, had crossed the little branch at the bottom of the hill and was about 200 yards away from us. Men rarely wore suits in those days, except to weddings or funerals, so he looked out of place all dressed up.

We didn't especially like to talk to strangers, so we decided to walk out into the cornfield among the fodder shocks until he passed. We gave the man time to go by, then came out and looked around, but the stranger in the gray suit was nowhere in sight. We had a good view of the road and the fields, but we saw no sign of him. He had simply vanished.

There were stories of other sightings near that branch. It was said that men used to meet there to gamble and, during one such meeting, a man was killed in a dispute. He was described as a man from out of town—a city fellow—wearing a gray suit. Others besides Dad, our neighbor, and me saw the man walking along that stretch of road, but he always vanished before anyone could get close to him.

Animal Ghosts

LB: When Lucian and Lena Brown were first married, they rented a small farm down Breckenridge Road off Highway 80 in Russell County. It came with a nice farmhouse and a barn that was located a little way off from the house. Since they had no livestock, they used the barn for storage. Nothing about the barn suggested anything scary or supernatural.

Shortly after they moved in, though, strange things began to happen. The couple had just gone to bed one night when they heard a terrible ruckus in the barn. It sounded like hogs fighting and squealing at full volume. Lucian and Lena were amazed by the sounds, because they had no hogs. A neighbor of theirs had hogs, but the barn doors were closed so that the neighbor's hogs couldn't have gotten in even if they got out of the neighbor's pen. But there was no denying that something was in the barn.

"What on earth is that?" Lena asked, sitting up in bed.

"I don't know," Lucian answered. "The neighbor's hogs must have gotten out and managed to get in our barn somehow. I'd better go and see what's going on."

Lucian grabbed his gun, and he and Lena ran to the barn. The loud fighting continued as they reached the barn door. Lucian pushed it open, expecting to confront angry animals, but to his amazement, nothing was there! The noise stopped abruptly as soon as he opened the door. He and Lena stepped inside and looked around, but there was no sign that any kind of animal had been there. Nothing was out of place. They searched all the stables and the storage area, but nothing was there that shouldn't have been. Puzzled, they returned to bed. The rest of the night was uneventful.

The nights that followed brought the same mysterious sounds from the barn. For the first few nights, when Lucian and Lena heard the loud squealing they'd go out to the barn to see if they could find the source. After a while, they stopped responding. They would just stay in bed and listen and, after a while, the noise would stop.

They told their neighbors what was happening. The neighbors told them that the landlord once kept hogs in the barn to fatten them up before he butchered them in the fall. Maybe the poor animals sensed their fate and were fighting for their lives. Lucian and Lena never got a better explanation than that.

Mammoth Cave

LB: One October several years ago, Roberta was hired to tell stories at Mammoth Cave State Park. I went along because the park is such an interesting place to visit. I talked to one of the guides while Roberta did her program.

The guide told me that Mammoth Cave has 330 miles of passageways on five levels, making it the largest system of caves in the world. It has been in operation for over 150 years and has had over 150 ghost sightings. It could be that Mammoth Cave is not only the biggest cave in the world, but also the most haunted.

The guide said that many visitors claim to have seen the ghost of Stephen Bishop, a black slave who began leading tours of the cave in 1838. Others think they have seen the ghost of a local girl named Melissa, who got revenge on the man who left her for another woman by abandoning him in the cave as a prank. When she went back to look for him, he had vanished and was never seen again. It is said that her ghost still looks for him. The guide related many other tales of ghostly voices, lights, and footprints.

"Those are great stories," I told him, "but did you ever see anything yourself that you couldn't explain?"

"There was one thing I'll never forget. I was standing on that bridge with another guide once," he said, pointing to the little overpass between the visitor's center and the restaurant and gift shop. "We were talking and looking at the trail below when we heard footsteps. We couldn't believe what came into view. I swear there was a pair of disembodied legs wearing boots and overalls! There was no body, but the legs just kept on walking out of sight. It was the weirdest thing I have ever seen!"

Ghost of Berea College

RB: As a 1963 graduate of Berea College in Berea, Kentucky, I am very proud that it has been recognized as one of the top academic schools in America. It is also noted for its labor program, which enables poor but promising students of Appalachia to work their way through college. Founded by John Gregg Fee in 1855, Berea traces its inspiration to Paul's words in the Book of Acts in the Bible, "God has made of one blood all peoples of the earth."

The college accepts a limited number of out-of-area students so the Appalachian students will be exposed to other cultures. In some cases, students were exposed to "other worlds," too.

Some have stories of strange things they have experienced in the Boone Tavern Hotel, which was once a part of the Underground Railroad. Several rooms in the basement were used to hide runaway slaves. It has been reported that voices can sometimes be heard and that there have been sightings of a young African American boy, about twelve years old, who appears to be frightened.

My own ghostly experience happened in a different location. Much of my world in the early 1960s was centered on the Tabernacle, the campus theater popularly known as the Tab. The theater did one weekly one-act play and a major three-act production each semester. As an English major, I was deeply involved in all aspects of the productions. Rehearsals for the fall production were going on when I had a strange encounter.

While rehearsing in the Tab, we all joked about cold breezes, creaking noises, and maybe the feeling that something had just brushed against us in passing, but we usually shrugged it off as normal happenings in a drafty old building.

In addition to participating in extracurricular activities and keeping up with academic studies, each student at Berea had to work from ten to twenty-four hours a week. My job was to be a live-in babysitter for the two children of the college's Dean of Guidance and his wife, who was the college psychiatrist. Both had been called out early one evening to deal with students' problems, and their daughter was playing with a friend next door, when I realized I needed a script I'd left at the Tab. I took their little boy, Chris, with me and we walked across campus to pick up the script.

Students were rehearsing on the stage inside the theater, but the office where the scripts were kept was open and deserted. Chris and I went in and, as I was signing out the script I needed, we heard loud, distinct footsteps come down the hall and stop outside the office door. Chris and I looked at the door to see who was coming in.

"Hi!" Chris said, but there was no answer.

I didn't see anyone, but I thought maybe Chris could see someone beside the door out of my range of vision.

"Who's there?" I asked.

"A man," Chris answered.

"Where is he?" I asked. "I don't see anybody."

"He's standing right there in the door," Chris insisted.

Chris definitely said *in* the door, not *beside* it.

Before I could say anything else, Chris added, "And he's wearing white boots."

Perhaps it was that last vivid detail that prompted movement in my frozen body. I grabbed my script and Chris and ran into the hallway. The ghost must have been prompted to move, too, because the sound of footsteps ahead of us faded away. There was nothing in the hallway with us. There was no place for anyone to hide, yet something had been there and vanished.

Afterward, I always wondered why Chris saw the apparition and I did not. We both heard the footsteps. Perhaps because he was a small child, Chris had a sensitivity that I had outgrown.

The Tab burned to the ground in 1973 and has since been replaced by a new drama center. I don't know if the ghosts left after the Tab was gone or if they remained to haunt the new center, too.

Night Caller

RB: One of the strangest experiences of my life involved a message that came to me in a dream and saved my sister's life. I was in Louisville, Kentucky, at the time and my sister, Fatima, was in Madison, Tennessee, but she heard me 164 miles away when I gave her a warning without using anything but my voice.

It happened one autumn night in the 1960s. I wrote about the experience and sold it to *Fate* magazine in the 1980s. *Fate* later published it in an anthology. In 2002, a producer for Lifetime TV's show *Beyond Chance* read it in the *Fate* anthology and thought it an intriguing story, so they filmed it for the show. It aired on Lifetime on March 4, 2002. With twenty years each between the happening, the writing, and the filming, I thought the timing was almost as strange as the story itself.

Just after I graduated from college I began teaching in Louisville, Kentucky. One evening I was out, directing a play at the high school where I taught. When I got home, my roommate was ironing, so I sat down to watch the eleven o'clock news with her.

Immediately, I fell into a light sleep and dreamed that a man was shaking the storm door. I could see him clearly. He was a short, stocky man with salt-and-pepper hair styled in a crew cut. I was suddenly very frightened. I woke myself screaming, "Don't open that door!"

I felt foolish when I realized what I had done. My roommate was staring at me, puzzled, because there was nobody trying to open our door. Then I realized that the door I had seen in my dream was the door of my sister's house in Madison, Tennessee. I had such an uneasy feeling about it that I finally had to call my sister to make sure she was all right before I could go back to sleep.

As soon as she heard my voice on the phone, my sister said, "You won't believe this. The strangest thing just happened!"

She explained that she was in the house alone because her husband was working second shift at the Ford Glass Plant and her son, Mike, was visiting some friends. She had told Mike to be home by ten o'clock. With the one-hour time difference between Madison and Louisville, it would have been eleven o'clock in Louisville. At ten o'clock, she heard someone start shaking her storm door.

My sister was a very trusting person who never hesitated to open her door to anybody. Thinking her son, Mike, was at the door, she started to open the door without first looking out to see who was there.

"Just then," she told me, "I heard your voice call out clearly, 'Don't open that door!'"

Of course, hearing my voice from out of nowhere startled her. Instead of opening the door as she had intended to do, she stopped and called out, "Mike?"

Evidently the person at the door thought she was calling for someone inside the house to come open the door instead of her. He stopped shaking the door, turned, and ran from the porch. She looked out and saw him running through the yard to the sidewalk. As he passed under the streetlight, she could see that he was a short, heavyset man with a graying crew cut.

We ended our call at that point, but she called me later to tell me the rest of the story.

A few minutes after our conversation, Mike's friends brought him home. They didn't want him to walk because they had heard on the radio that a murderer had escaped from the hospital for the criminally insane that was located just a couple of miles down the road. Authorities believed he was still in the area.

Fatima thanked Mike's friends for bringing him home, and they left. She and Mike sat down to watch TV until her husband came home from work. A bulletin flashed on the screen, showing the man my sister had seen running from her porch. He was the escaped killer, and he was captured on her street, just two houses down from hers.

We never figured out how she heard my voice 164 miles away. We do know that if she hadn't heard it, she would have opened her door that night to an insane killer.

Woman at the Spring

RB: When Henry Ashley heard that his neighbor's daughter had died, he went over to sit with the family. It was the custom for neighbors to bring food and help with whatever needed to be done, whether it was building a coffin or dressing the corpse. Henry had worked hard that day and was tired, but he did not want the family to be alone. He hadn't been at the neighbor's house long when others arrived, so Henry decided to go home and get some sleep.

The bright moonlight made it seem like day as he walked along. It was a good thing the moon was so bright because

Henry had not brought a lantern. He hadn't planned to walk home until morning, but he could see well in the moonlight even without a lantern.

As Henry approached the house of another neighbor, Mr. Sullivan, his energy rose because he knew at that point he was halfway home. He increased his pace because the autumn air was suddenly turning colder.

The spring where the Sullivan family got water was located by the side of the road. As Henry drew near, he saw a woman in a long white gown standing on the other side of the spring. When he looked closer, he saw that it was Mr. Sullivan's wife, Marge.

At first, Henry wasn't too surprised to see someone at the spring. If anybody got sick at night, someone in the family would usually rush to the spring for fresh, cool water for the sick person to drink. He thought that was what had happened. Then it occurred to him that it was unlikely that Mrs. Sullivan would have come out on a chilly autumn night wearing only a nightgown. *Maybe she was sleepwalking,* he thought.

"Is everything all right?" he called to her.

She shook her head and vanished!

Henry was stunned by this turn of events. Had he really seen someone there or was it a trick of the moonlight? He looked down toward the Sullivans' house, but there was no light. He didn't want to go wake them up and tell them what he thought he had seen. They would think he was crazy. He decided to hurry on home and keep his experience to himself. Maybe he needed sleep more than he thought if he were seeing things.

The next morning, while Henry and his family were having breakfast, there was a knock at the door. Henry's wife, Lucy, opened the door to see who was there so early. It was one of the Sullivan girls, and she was crying.

"What's wrong, child?" Lucy asked.

"Momma died in her sleep last night," the girl sobbed. "Poppa wants to know if you can come and help dress her."

"Of course," Lucy told her. "I am so sorry!"

Lucy left with the girl to do what she could for the family. When she returned later, Henry had one question.

"What was Marge wearing when she died?" he wanted to know.

"A long white nightgown," Lucy answered. "Why do you ask?"

The Ghost of JCC

RB: In the fall of 1998, I was writing an article about local haunted sites for *Louisville Magazine.* I'd heard stories about many strange happenings at Jefferson Community College, so I interviewed the security chief about the reports.

I learned that the building was constructed over a hundred years ago as the Louisville Presbyterian Seminary. In the library on the second floor, there is an inscription over the fireplace: *This building was erected by James Rankin Barret in loving memory of his wife, Lucy Sites Barret.* It is only fitting that

Lucy should haunt this room. The ghost was so active that the head of security kept a file documenting all the happenings his officers reported.

"People hear footsteps when nobody is there," he told me. "The elevator goes up and down on its own, carrying no visible passengers. Lights flicker and dim when storms and power surges can't be blamed. Doorknobs turn by unseen hands, and some employees have reported seeing a figure in the hall. Two cleaning ladies were so scared by the spooky presence that they quit their jobs. Mysterious letters, supposedly from the ghost, are left in various places. The last one was left in the chapel near Halloween last year. It was signed with the initials LBS and announced 'I am still with you.'"

The guard had an incident of his own to add to his file in 1980.

He was working the shift between midnight and dawn. He'd made his rounds, making sure the windows and doors were secure. With new batteries in his flashlight, he moved through the dark, silent halls following a routine inspection. Then it happened.

"I entered the Records and Admissions Office about 3:00 A.M.," he said. "Suddenly, my flashlight dimmed and I felt a cold draft on the back of my neck. I got this prickling sensation up and down my spine. I had an overwhelming feeling that there was a presence in the room with me."

He believed the ghost was Lucy, but he didn't think she was there to harm anyone.

When I finished writing my article, the magazine sent

its photographer, John Nation, to go with me back to the college to photograph the different sites. John is an excellent photographer, so I was excited by the prospect of being able to watch him work.

We entered the library at JCC, and John put one of his cameras on a chair across the room from the fireplace. Then, holding another camera, he approached the fireplace to photograph the inscription about Lucy. He was puzzled when the camera wouldn't work. It had been working fine up until then. Just then, the camera on the chair across the room from us began to flash on its own!

I began to feel that we were not the only ones in that room. John tried and tried before he was able to get the camera to work and take the pictures he wanted. As soon as he did, we grabbed all of the photographic equipment and made a hasty exit.

The Spurlington Witch

RB: What is autumn without a good witch story? I grew up less than fifty miles from Taylor County's Spurlington community, but I have to admit I'd never heard of the Spurlington Witch until my friend and former teacher, the late Dr. Drewry Meece Jr., sent me a newspaper clipping from the *Central Kentucky News-Journal* in October 2002. Another friend and school chum, Ola May (Foley) Martin, later supplied more information. I was fascinated with what I heard about the witch. Many stories have been handed down over the years and, true or not true, the legend of Kentucky's Spurlington Witch persists.

The woman thought to be a witch was Nancy Bass. The 1850 U.S. Census confirms that she was a real person who lived in Campbellsville, Kentucky. All the sources I consulted suggest that she was an outcast, and people feared she would cast spells on them if they crossed her. Any mysterious illness or bad luck was blamed on her.

The most prominent story about Nancy is that she witnessed a group of train robbers (some say the group was led by Jesse James) burying some gold they had stolen in a train robbery. They saw her watching, so they killed her and buried her with the treasure somewhere on the top of the Spurlington Tunnel. There is no grave marker, and treasure hunters who have scoured the area have not found the body or the gold.

People say that the witch cursed her killers and all who pass though the tunnel. It is also said that a woman, believed to be the witch, sometimes appears in photos taken at the tunnel entrance.

The 1,900-foot-long tunnel located eight miles north of Campbellsville is no longer in use. Whether there really is a Spurlington Witch may never be known. Most people would not want to risk crossing her path to find out.

The Cat's Meow

LB: In the fall of 2006, a friend of ours said he had been invited to tour a hundred-year-old haunted house about an hour's drive out of Louisville. The owners had told him that he was welcome to bring guests, so he asked if we would like to join him. We eagerly accepted his invitation. We knew no details about the haunted house, but that made it more interesting. We have always preferred not to know about sites we visit.

The owners said they would meet us there about six o'clock, but we arrived before they did. We parked by the side of the house to wait and look at the house and its surroundings.

"I'm sure they'll be here soon," our friend commented.

I was looking up at a second-floor window when a woman came up to the window and looked out.

"Somebody's already here," I said. "I see a woman looking at us from the second-floor window."

Roberta looked up and said, "Oh, yeah, I see her. She's wearing a white, high-necked dress and has dark hair pulled back."

Her description matched what I was seeing. We continued to watch for three or four minutes. The woman would move away from the window and then come back and look out again. It seemed to us that she was trying to figure out who we were and what we were doing there.

When the owners arrived, we told them that someone was in the house. We explained how we had been watching her watching us.

"Was it that window?" one of the owners asked, pointing to the exact window we had been watching.

We nodded. The owners laughed.

"That's just our ghost, Aileen," said the other owner. "She once said out loud to me, 'I am Aileen, with an A!'"

Excited about the sighting, we followed the owners inside the house and started the tour. We were in the hall when we suddenly heard, *"Meow!"* It was so loud and close that we turned around to see the cat. To our surprise, there was no cat.

"That's our ghost cat," explained one of the owners.

"Meow!" it said again, as if it were right there on the floor. Evidently, that second "Meow" meant good-bye, because we did not hear the cat again.

The other owner explained that the house was once owned by a man who had a large family to feed. From the information the owners were able to gather, they learned that the man would not allow animals in the house because it was hard enough to feed the humans in his family. The lady of the house (maybe Aileen, but they didn't know) would sneak food outside to her cat until the woman died. Perhaps the cat starved after that, because the ghost cat arrived at the house shortly after the lady's death. Maybe it thought it could live in the house once it became invisible.

School Visitor

RB: My Uncle George Simpson was one of my favorite people in the world. He was sheriff of Adair County for many years and lived about twelve miles from us. We had no car, so it was especially thrilling for my sister and me when he took us for a ride in his police car and let us turn on the siren. We lived so far out in the country that the siren didn't bother anybody.

Uncle George was a great believer in education. He was disappointed when his own children chose not to go to college. He was especially proud of me because I became a teacher.

I visited Uncle George just days before he died, and once I got back to Louisville I decided not to drive back for the funeral. I was preparing my students for an important test, and I didn't want to miss school. While Uncle George's funeral was taking place in Russell County, I was conducting my ninth-grade English class on the second floor of what was then Southern Junior High School. My students knew that my uncle had died, but I had not dwelt on the subject. We were concentrating on our work.

I had moved Ralph, one of my mischievous students, to a seat at the front of the room facing the door to keep him out of trouble. The door and windows were closed, and all the students were seated.

Suddenly, Ralph pointed at the door and said, "Look!"

It didn't look like he was trying to distract us. Ralph looked scared.

We all looked at the door as the doorknob turned and the door swung open. Then it closed and clicked, as if someone had come in and pushed it shut behind him. The glass panes in the door gave us an excellent view of the hall beyond, and we could see that nobody was there. There was no draft from the closed windows, yet some papers fell off desks, untouched by students, as someone, or something, seemed to walk around the room. None of us moved or made a sound. Then the classroom door opened and closed again by itself, as if our unseen visitor had gone out.

"What was that?" Ralph asked.

I shook my head. I was at a loss for words, but one girl spoke up.

"That could have been your Uncle George," she said. "Since you couldn't go say good-bye to him, maybe he came to say good-bye to you. You said he liked school."

Maybe she was right. We never found a better identity for our invisible school visitor.

The Widow Hoag

RB: A spirit might remain earthbound because it can't accept its own death or because someone can't accept the death of a loved one. The latter seems to have been the case with a widow named Hoag who lived in a third-floor apartment on Fountain Court in Old Louisville during World War II.

"My mother, Pat, lived in the same building as a child," said Bob, whom I interviewed about his experience, "and she remembers the day the news came that Mrs. Hoag's son was killed trying to land his plane on an aircraft carrier. It was so tragic! They never found the body, so Mrs. Hoag refused to believe her son was dead. She was sure he'd come home someday, so she insisted she would have to stay there so he could find her."

Pat eventually grew up and moved away, but the widow stayed on, waiting and waiting for her lost son. She believed until the day she died that her son would return to her.

In 1980, Pat moved with her two sons into the renovated apartment where the Widow Hoag had lived. One son, Bob, the man who told me the story, would soon witness an apparition from another time and place.

Bob was a teenager when it happened, but he still has vivid memories of the encounter.

"I was enjoying having the apartment all to myself for the first time since we had moved in," he said. "I'd just had a shower without anybody beating on the door, and I had walked into the bedroom wearing a robe when I saw it. A movement at one of the wraparound windows caught my eye. I knew it couldn't be a neighbor because we were up too high. I stood there, terrified, as I watched the blackened outline of an old woman glide across the floor into a blank wall. I don't know how long I stood there or how I got out of my robe. The next thing I knew, I was outside our back door, trying to stuff my still-damp legs into my jeans.

"I was shivering, and I knew I had to get out of there. Since I had no car, I had to call someone to come and get me. Fortunately, the phone cord stretched out the back door. I leaned against it as I shakily dialed Mother at her friend's house. She seemed unconcerned when I told her what I had seen."

Bob's mother thought he was joking when he first called. He'd never been afraid of anything, but she slowly realized he was badly frightened now. She told him to get some clothes on if he was going to wait outside in the autumn air.

"I made her stay on the line while I went back inside and finished dressing," Bob said.

"You know who it is," she told Bob later. "It's the Widow Hoag. She thinks you are her lost son who's come back home."

The house is still there on Fountain Court. Bob is sure the Widow Hoag is still there, too.

The Brennan House

LB: The Brennan House, located at 631 South Fifth Street in Louisville, Kentucky, was built in 1868. In 1884, Thomas Brennan purchased the house and moved in with his wife and nine children. Some say they loved the house so much that they stayed on even after death.

One autumn day, we took a private tour with our friend, Robert Parker, and learned some fascinating stories about the Brennan House from one of the guides.

In the parlor are three portraits of Mr. and Mrs. Brennan, two of which are portraits of Mrs. Brennan at different ages. We noticed that they were hanging crookedly on the wall. The guide, straightening them as he spoke, said these portraits are often the subject of paranormal activity.

"When I open up in the morning," said the guide, "I sometimes find them tilted to the right, sometimes to the left, or sometimes just crooked like this."

One Brennan son was a doctor and had an office downstairs adjacent to the front of the house. The staff often smells the faint odor of cigars, which the doctor enjoyed smoking.

As we walked through the office, we could smell the lingering odor, too. The mystery is the source of the smoke, because the house is a no-smoking facility.

Upstairs, the guide showed us a cradle that he has seen rocking by itself. When he was closing one night, he heard a loud clicking sound and looked down the hall to see the cradle rocking wildly from side to side. Nobody else was around. He ran to get another guide, and the two stood watching it until it slowed down and stopped on its own. They learned that baby Napoleon Brennan had a stomach disorder that was often soothed by rocking the cradle faster than normal.

Napoleon married very late in life and expected to move his new wife into the Brennan House. Mysterious voices and the sound of the piano playing by itself were so disturbing to her upon entering that she would not remain there and returned to her former home. Napoleon soon followed and lived with her there, leaving the Brennan House to stand empty, as it does to this day.

Robert Parker, also known as Mr. Ghost Walker, leads a ghost walk downtown past the Brennan House. Once in a while, a ghost will make an appearance at a window as the tour goes by.

Pope Lick Monster

RB: My students at Pleasure Ridge Park High School in Louisville were the first to tell me about the Pope Lick Monster when I began teaching in 1963. It seemed that every teenager in Jefferson County knew about the monster and wanted to get a look at it. Tales of the creature have been told for decades, but they are especially popular around Halloween. Is it true or just an urban legend?

People say that the monster lives below a train trestle that passes over Pope Lick Road and Pope Lick Creek out Taylorsville Road. This trestle spans nearly 800 feet and is about 100 feet tall. The trestle is of more concern to officials than the monster because there have been numerous accidents and deaths involving people who have dared to walk on the trestle. Getting hit by a train is probably more likely than getting caught by a monster.

Descriptions of what this monster looks like vary. Some say he is half man, half goat or sheep, with horns, hooves, and a hairy body. Some say he is an old chemist, disfigured in an explosion. Others believe he is a freak animal that a circus found in the Canadian wilderness and lost at the trestle during a violent thunderstorm when lightning struck the train. And there are those who believe he is only a hermit, or maybe a headless horseman, who rides the train tracks and chases all that cross his path. There have been very few sightings of the monster, if any, so what it is (if it truly exists at all) remains a mystery.

In 1988 Ron Schildknecht released a film called *The Pope Lick Monster*. He admitted that, although he did not see the monster, he found the place a little frightening.

I have to agree with him. A few years ago, I was going to do a storytelling program in the Jeffersontown area. I was thinking about which stories to tell when I suddenly realized I was driving through the Pope Lick Monster's territory. Trees lined the narrow road and cast strange shadows. I could almost imagine the monster lurking there beside the road. It was a very spooky place! I stepped on the gas a little more until I was out of the monster's boundaries. I had the strangest feeling that something was watching me as I sped away.

Hot Rod Haven

LB: I first heard of Hot Rod Haven when I moved to Louisville in the 1950s. Roberta's high school students talked about the place when she started teaching in the 1960s. Through the years, the story of the haunted site persisted and captured the imagination of teenagers in the area.

Located on Mitchell Hill Road in south Louisville, Hot Rod Haven was a favorite place for teenagers to park. The road has lots of curves that allowed teenage drivers to test their hot rods, and that was how the spot got its name. Lots of people lost their lives on this twisting road over the years.

At the top of the hill is a cemetery that is said to be haunted. Many driving by have reported seeing a ghostly figure roaming around among the graves.

Legend has it that a couple, Roy Clarke and Sarah Mitchell, were on their way to a school dance on September 23, 1946, when Roy lost control of his car. They swerved around the twisting curves and crashed at the bottom of the hill. The two young people were pronounced dead at the scene. They are buried in the cemetery on the hill; their marker is a single stone.

Many believe that the ghostly figure seen in the cemetery is Sarah's ghost. She is wearing the same dress that she had on for the dance.

Iroquois Park Ghost

LB: Iroquois Park in Louisville, Kentucky, has seen a number of grisly murders over the years. You'd think that victims of recent violent deaths would haunt their murder site, but that does not seem to be the case. Most reports are of seeing the ghost of a headless woman, especially near the lookout point at the top of the 250-foot tree-covered knob in the park.

Some park visitors who come to see the autumn leaves say they have experienced a thick fog that comes rolling in suddenly. This is followed by the sound of a barking dog and the smell of smoke. Then a woman dressed in clothes from the 1800s walks from the mist, holding her head in her hands while the blood drips from her neck.

The story of the woman's death goes back to the 1800s when she and her farmer-husband settled in the area that is now Iroquois Park. One night while her husband was in town on business, she was at home alone with the family dog when Indians attacked the homestead. They slit the dog's throat to silence it, rushed in, and beheaded the helpless woman before ransacking the house. Before leaving, the Indians set fire to the house to try to cover up what they had done. This would account for the eerie barking sounds, the smell of smoke, and the headless ghost that visitors claim to see.

The Belle of Louisville

RB: Officially the *Belle of Louisville* is not haunted. The owners deny all such claims, probably because they are concerned about the adverse effect ghosts might have on business. I've had an opportunity to be on board the magnificent old paddle-wheel steamboat "after hours," however, and my experiences there have left me wondering. Talks with members of the crew who have to remain anonymous because of concern over their jobs confirm that my feelings might have some validity.

The *Belle of Louisville* was built by James Rees & Sons in 1914 and was first known as the *Idlewild.* It first operated as a ferry and day packet, carrying passengers, freight, farm produce, and even livestock. In 1928, the New St. Louis and Calhoun Packet Corporation of Hardin, Illinois, bought the steamboat and used it for a single season as a New Orleans excursion boat. After that, it changed ownership several times. It went to St. Louis for a time to work on the Illinois River. The Rose Island Company chartered the ship in 1931 after they lost the steamer *America.* In 1934, the *Idlewild* replaced Louisville's excursion boat, the *City of Memphis,* and continued to be in service as an excursion boat until World

War II. During the war, the *Idlewild* towed oil barges. After the war, it went back to being an excursion boat. In 1947, J. Herod Gorsage of Peoria, Illinois, bought the *Idlewild,* and Captain Ben Winters became her master.

Many stories of the dark side of Captain Winters abound. Perhaps these are just stories, but there are many accusations of the captain's cruelty against his crew and of illegal activities. He had previously worked on a packet called the *Avalon* and his death wish to change the name of the *Idlewild* to the *Avalon* was granted. He died in the captain's quarters on the steamboat.

In 1949, the *Avalon* was sold to parties in Cincinnati, Ohio, and traveled the western rivers until 1962, when it was sold at auction to Jefferson County, Kentucky, for $34,000. The steamboat underwent extensive restoration and opened on April 30, 1963, as the *Belle of Louisville.*

One night in late September 2004 a group from the Mid South Paranormal Conference was on board the *Belle of Louisville,* and my friend Robert Parker took a picture of the captain's quarters. He looked at his picture and showed it to me. To our amazement, there on the wall was a distinct face that we had not seen when we were in the room. A crew member told us that lots of people get that face in their pictures of the captain's quarters—the face of Captain Winters! The crew member told us that some visitors have seen a face in the mirror in the women's bathroom, too, but it has not been identified.

Lights also went on and off for no apparent reason while

we were in the captain's quarters. We learned later that lights often blink when the captain's ghost is believed to be present.

Robert and I were interested in the steamboat's history, but we also wanted to see if we could find out more about any paranormal activities on board. We left the group and wandered into what used to be the sick bay. We didn't see anything in there except a very expensive-looking ring. Robert picked it up and handed it to me. We immediately felt deeply depressed. It was such a strong feeling that we both felt we had to get out of there at once. We put the ring back on the narrow ledge where we found it and hurried from that room to the deck area beside the calliope.

"I'm so cold!" exclaimed Robert.

I began to feel the same way. It was not the chill of an autumn night on the Ohio River. It was a bone-penetrating cold that left us almost immobile.

"This cold isn't normal," I said.

"Something happened here," Robert declared. "Something really bad."

I nodded in agreement. I felt it, too. It was so bad that I just wanted to get away from that spot.

"Let's join the others," I suggested.

Robert nodded and we hurried back to the group. We saw a guide, and Robert asked him if anything bad had ever happened near the calliope. We were not surprised at his answer.

"Yes, it did," he said. "Years ago, two deck hands got in a fight. One killed the other right there near the calliope."

It was the very spot where Robert and I had felt the bone-chilling cold.

The Palace Theater

RB: I learned about the Palace Theater from two friends of mine, Robert Parker and Jay Gravette. Robert carefully researched the Palace for his walking ghost tour and his book *Haunted Louisville*. Jay has first-hand information from his grandfather, Ferdinand Frisch, who worked in the theater for forty years and died there in his office of a massive heart attack on October 27, 1965. Many believe that Ferdinand's ghost haunts the Palace.

Anyone, living or dead, would enjoy being in this grand theater. This $1.2 million building, designed by John Eberson, opened first as Loew's Theater on September 1, 1928. It went through several changes in name and construction in the years that followed. In the 1950s, its name was changed to United Artists Theater. Other renovations followed through the years, and the theater eventually emerged in the 1990s as the Palace. A unique feature of the Palace is the lobby's ceiling, which contains busts of 130 historic figures.

Many people claim the Palace is haunted. There are accounts of a ghostly woman on the stairs, children giggling in the women's restroom, and the sound of running feet. Workmen's tools are mysteriously moved about, and some have reported seeing an elderly man sitting in the balcony. Others claim to have seen the ghost of Ferdinand Frisch in the basement. Still others say they have seen the ghost of another man, a projectionist named Barney, who worked and died in the theater in the 1930s.

It must have been difficult working in the projection booth without air-conditioning, but Barney carried out his duties faithfully. One day, he suffered a heart attack while working in the booth, but that is not what killed him. Well-meaning rescuers tried to carry him down the stairs, using a door as a makeshift stretcher. They tripped on the steps and dropped the door—and Barney. The drop was what killed Barney.

Both Ferdinand and Barney were dedicated to their work in the theater; perhaps both still return to the place they cared about in life. In any case, I can say from experience that there is a male ghost in the Palace; I saw it with my own eyes.

On the weekend of September 22–24, 2006, the Mid South Paranormal Conference was held in Louisville, Kentucky. Rain poured on Louisville that weekend, flooding many areas of the city, but it failed to dampen the spirits of those of us who took part in the many exciting events. The rainy night added a spooky touch to our ghost-hunting activities.

Keith Age, founder and leader of the Louisville Ghost Hunter's Society, had just finished filming a movie, *Spooked*, about the Waverly Hills Sanatorium. The premiere of this movie was held at the Palace Theater on Saturday night, September 23. In connection with that premiere, the Palace allowed the general public to pay a fee, which would allow them to spend the night in the spooky theater. Participants were divided into groups and allowed to explore all areas of the theater with guides.

I was in a group with my friend, Linda, and we rotated with the other groups through the building. A little after 2:00 A.M., we found ourselves having to wait for a short time in the bar area while another group finished at our next location. Linda and I sat down at one of the tables to rest and chat. We weren't talking about ghosts at that point. We were talking about other places we'd like to visit. Suddenly, we saw a mist forming. The dark form of a man materialized and moved quickly past us. It didn't walk. It seemed to float. Linda and I stopped talking and looked at each other.

"Did you see that?" she asked.

"You mean that big dark thing that just went by us?" I answered.

She nodded, and we compared notes. We had both seen the same thing. Since it was in the area where the ghost of Barney has been seen, we decided it might have been the projectionist putting in an appearance.

Waverly Hills Sanatorium

RB: Waverly Hills Sanatorium has been described as one of the scariest places on earth. Movies, television shows, and documentaries have been made about it. People from everywhere come to Louisville, Kentucky, to take tours through the place. Anyone who visits Waverly Hills Sanatorium is likely to come away with some stories of strange happenings that can't be explained. Lonnie and I are no exceptions. We have certainly encountered some eerie things there.

The sanatorium is a sinister-looking monster of a building sitting high on a hill overlooking south Louisville. It was established in 1910 as a two-story wooden building that served as a hospital with forty beds.

In 1900, Louisville had the highest tuberculosis death rate in the country, mainly because its swampy land was a perfect breeding ground for the bacteria that caused the deadly disease. Dying from tuberculosis was not an easy death. The disease caused sufferers' lungs to burn and victims to choke and gasp for air. In those days, there was no cure for tuberculosis. Some patients did survive, but many did not.

It was hoped that the isolated location of the sanatorium, along with the fresh air and the latest treatments known to medical science at that time would be able to stop, or at least contain, the spread of this killer disease. However, it soon became evident that the little hospital was not enough. As more and more patients needed treatment, more space was needed.

Construction of a new hospital began in 1924, and the new facility was opened in 1926. It consisted of five floors, the fifth floor, smaller than the others, reserved for mental patients who had the dreaded disease.

Even with what was then considered state-of-the-art treatment, thousands died within Waverly's walls. Experimental surgery was performed to try to bring relief, and patients were exposed to fresh air even in winter. Photographs show patients on the balcony with snow on their bed covers. None of these things were done to be cruel to patients. These were things that the best doctors truly believed would help. In spite of the staff's good intentions, however, the deaths continued.

To prevent patients from having to see the bodies of their fellows who died, a body chute (which became known as the Death Tunnel) was built to transport bodies from the hospital morgue to the railroad tracks at the bottom of the hill. In bad weather, workers who lived outside the hospital used the Death Tunnel as a walkway up the hill to work.

With the discovery of the antibiotic streptomycin, tuberculosis was wiped out for the most part by the mid-1950s. Waverly Hills Sanatorium was no longer needed, so it closed in 1961.

In 1962, the facility was reopened, this time as the Woodhaven Geriatrics Sanitarium. Conditions and treatments were so horrible there that the commonwealth of Kentucky closed it in 1982 because of patient abuse. The horror of what happened to these patients could be added to the horror of all the thousands who died of tuberculosis behind these walls.

Waverly Hills changed hands several times over the next eighteen years. One owner wanted the building torn down so he could build the largest statue of Jesus in the world. He was refused permission to tear it down because the facility was on the historic register, so he decided to let others come in and destroy it. During those years, the place was completely vandalized.

In 2001, Charles and Tina Mattingly purchased the buildings and property. They allow tours and hope eventually to restore the building.

With the suffering, death, and abuse that occurred behind its walls, it is little wonder that Waverly Hills had gained the reputation of being one of the most haunted sites in the world.

In September 2003, during the Mid South Paranormal Conference, Lonnie and I had our first chance to tour Waverly with other authors, including Troy Taylor, Dave Goodwin, and Alan Brown. Keith Age, president of the Louisville Ghost Hunters, was our group's guide for the night. We had barely entered the building when startling things began to happen.

Lonnie and I were in line close behind Keith. As we reached the top of the first flight of stairs, a thick and heavy metal door opened a little on its own and slammed shut with tremendous force right in our faces. It took all of us by surprise, but we recovered and continued on. The door opened normally when Keith took hold of it, and there was nobody on the other side.

Some teenage boys were not so lucky a few years ago. They managed to sneak past security and enter one of the rooms. They had carried an axe with them, though the reason for that was not made clear to me. Maybe they intended to do damage, or maybe they thought of it as some form of protection. When they tried to get out, they were surprised to find that the door wouldn't open. They thought at first that the door was just stuck, so they kept pushing on it. Regardless of how hard they pushed, it wouldn't budge. At that point, they panicked. The boy with the axe began beating the door as hard as he could, but still it wouldn't open. Suddenly, they were surrounded by shadows that got between them and the door and wouldn't let them out. The boys no longer worried about being caught trespassing. They just wanted to get out. They began screaming for help as loudly as they could. Two security guards heard the ruckus and rushed to the room. They opened the door easily. It wasn't stuck and offered no resistance at all!

We entered the second-floor hallway where the kitchen used to be. Sometimes the smell of bread baking fills this hallway, but on this night we smelled nothing surprising. The kitchen was empty and quiet. As we walked down the hallway, we noticed that rain had blown in through some broken windows and had puddled on the floor. With flash-lights and camera lights focused on the puddle (there was no electricity above the first floor), we were amazed to see wet footprints of bare feet walk out of the puddle and take several steps. Then they stopped. All of us were wearing shoes and standing well away from the puddle. We stared at the footprints until they faded away.

As we continued our tour, something unseen touched a member of our group on the back. On the third and fourth floors, we observed what is called "the shadow people" at Waverly. The shadowy forms showed no indication that they knew we were there. To us, they looked like nurses moving in and out of rooms, as if they were still treating patients.

On tours of Waverly we took later, more dramatic things happened. We saw faces looking out of windows when security was certain the building was empty. We also saw lifelike figures outside on the ground, but when security guards followed them, they simply vanished before their eyes. The face of a beautiful lady appeared in a photo between two members of our group where no real person could possibly have been standing. There was no way the face could have been a reflection.

Voices whispered in hallways and the Death Tunnel. Once, as we were walking through the tunnel, we heard a voice say, "Get out!" Then one of our group felt a tug at her hair even though she was last in line and there was nobody behind her.

Bits of the wall actually flew across the room and struck Keith Age when he was conducting tours. Once a bottle flew from a pile of trash in the corner as if flung by unseen hands.

People sometimes see lights in the building's elevator shafts, but there are no longer lights or elevators there. We were told that a homeless man and his dog fell down one of the elevator shafts and died. Some say they have seen the ghost of the dog.

Children as well as adults were patients at Waverly, and they often played on the roof of the fifth floor so they could get sunshine and fresh air.

A little boy who died at Waverly often rolled his little blue ball out during tours at various locations through the building. He must have been lonely and longed for someone to play with. Some visitors who saw the ball roll out rolled it back as if they were playing with the child. They were surprised to see it roll back to them again. Sometimes a child's laugh could be heard after incidents like this. Security guards have placed the ball in empty rooms, only to go back later and find it gone. They knew nobody had entered the rooms because they had been watching outside.

In the fall of 2004, during the Mid South Paranormal Conference, I was one of the guides who led groups on an overnight tour through Waverly. Most groups were made up of ten people, but my group consisted of seventeen American Ghost Hunters because their group wanted to tour the sanatorium together. All groups had a "caboose person" at the end of the line to keep anyone from wandering off. Because my group was so large, we also had a security guard with us to help out.

The groups rotated through the building throughout the night. During the course of the night we experienced many unusual things. Voices whispered, shadow people appeared, and group members felt the touch of invisible things that seemed to be walking beside us.

We checked out Room 502, which is considered by some to be the most haunted room in the hospital. A nurse is said to have committed suicide by hanging herself there. Members of our group came away with different feelings after entering the room. I only felt a drop in temperature, but one man backed out of the door so quickly that he almost stepped on me. He said he had never had such a hard time breathing in his life! Others had breathing problems, too, but nothing that extreme. Everyone in the room felt the intense cold in 502 that night.

There were no bathrooms in the building, since vandals had destroyed them all. Whenever someone in the group wanted to go to the bathroom, everybody in that group had to go outside the building to the port-a-potties. We had been instructed never to let the groups separate. Almost every time we went outside, someone would decide they'd had enough and that they wanted to go home. It kept me, my caboose, and the security person busy counting to make sure that everybody who was supposed to be present was actually there.

Sometime around 3:00 A.M. a person in my group needed to make a bathroom run. We decided to count heads before we went out to make sure no one had wandered off. On the floor we were on, the outer rooms had two doors. One led to the balcony walkway and one led to the inner corridor.

"I'll check the inner hallway," my caboose person said. "You take the balcony and we'll meet at the end of the building."

"Great," I said, and I asked the security guard to take the group to the end location to wait.

The guard and the group left, and the caboose person and I started checking the rooms. I could see from the balcony through the two doors to the inner hallway.

As I looked into one room, I saw the back of my caboose person pass the inner door. Then a figure materialized in the corner of the room and glided out the door, turning in the direction my caboose person had just gone. It looked like someone dressed in a white hospital coat, the kind a doctor would wear. The figure looked so real that I actually thought we had missed somebody. I stepped back and looked again, but the room was empty. I figured whoever it was had met up with my caboose person.

I hurried on down the balcony walkway to rejoin my group. Just as I got there, my caboose person came hurrying around the corner from the inner hall.

"Oh, my goodness!" she said. "Something just followed me down the hall! It was something wearing a white top!"

When we compared notes, it was obvious that we both had seen the same thing. Neither of us had felt threatened by the apparition, but it did make us feel uneasy.

PART IV
GHOSTS OF WINTER

Some people only think of ghosts at Halloween, but Halloween has not always been the traditional time for ghost stories. It used to be Christmas. Each year we read the beloved classic Christmas ghost story, *A Christmas Carol*, by Charles Dickens. In nineteenth-century England, Dickens would run contests to see who could write the best Christmas ghost story. Kentuckians would have done well in those contests because Kentucky has some of the best stories and storytellers in the world.

We lived in a small farming community in our younger years with no electricity, cell phones, texting, I-Pods, television, DVDs, or personal computers to fill our leisure time. In those days, relatives and friends did not just visit for hours; they often stayed for days. Travel was slower and more difficult then. We loved these long visits from friends and relations, and we would all gather around on cold winter nights and entertain ourselves with scary stories.

The winter solstice was not connected in our minds to

ancient rites or cultures. To us, it was just the shortest day of the year and signaled that spring was on its way.

Candles and lamplight were beautiful, but they also served the practical purpose of giving us light to read and move around. They also cast flickering shadows that provided the perfect backdrop for our spooky tales. More than any other time, winter, and the stories we told then, reminded us of the closeness of darkness and light and the eternal circle of life. Winter stories hold special memories for us, and we hope they will bring memories of stories of your own.

Haunted Seelbach Hotel

LB: One of the charms of living in the country was the arrival of unexpected guests on dark winter days. This usually meant that good food and ghost stories would be shared around a bright, crackling fire.

Sometimes hotels get unexpected guests in the dead of winter, too. According to Larry Johnson, bell captain at the Seelbach Hotel in Louisville, two ghostly guests entered there one night.

"About midnight on a very cold night in 1983," Johnson said, "a man cleaning the café inside the Seelbach saw a reflection in one of the mirrors. He stopped his cleaning and looked closer. The reflection was of an old woman dressed in ragged clothes as a bag lady might dress over by the door. She looked weary and chilled, so he thought he'd finish his work and let her have time to get warm before asking her to leave. After the cleaning person finished, he turned toward the door, but she was gone. He thought she had probably just gone back outside, but he reported it to security anyway. Security found no trace of the old lady either inside or outside the hotel.

Nothing else happened until 1985. Again, it was a cold winter night. All the guests were settled in, happy to be sheltered from the biting wind. Nobody stirred except for those working the late shift—and one more.

"Another man was working this time," said Johnson. "He caught sight of an old woman in the mirror and, like the first man, he felt sorry for her and decided to let her stay and get warm."

The results of this second encounter were the same. When the man turned to the spot where the old lady had been standing, he was shocked to find her gone. She appeared too frail to move very quickly, so the man called security to find her. Their search came up empty. Then one guard remembered the incident back in 1983.

"The sightings were identical," Johnson said, "but the two men who saw the old woman had never met each other."

The café was later remodeled and the mirror taken down. Since then, the old lady has not been seen.

Snowman

RB: Perhaps ghosts like to come inside on snowy nights, just as we humans do. I think I once had a visit from one.

In the winter of 1968, I was a single teacher living alone in a first-floor apartment in Louisville. Snow had fallen steadily all day one Saturday, and by nightfall, several inches had accumulated. It was definitely not a night to be outside, so I settled down with a good book and looked forward to a peaceful evening. Nobody went in or out of my apartment building, so the snow was pure and unbroken.

Just as I got comfortable and involved in my reading, I heard the outside door open, followed by heavy footsteps in the entrance hall by my apartment. The visitor stomped his feet, as if trying to get snow off his boots. Then he began beating on my door. It wasn't a gentle knock; it was definitely a pounding!

This unnerved me. None of my friends would beat hard enough to make the door shake, but this person was doing just that! I tiptoed to my door and looked through the peephole. I couldn't see anyone out there, but the knocking stopped. I heard heavy footsteps going toward the entrance, and then I heard the creak of the outside door opening. The footsteps went out and the door closed.

I ran to my front window and pulled back the drapes. The outside apartment lights were on, so I had a clear view of the entire front area. There was nobody anywhere to be seen. I looked down to see where the tracks led, but there were no tracks. The snow had not been touched. Nothing was stirring outside, not even the wind.

I talked to a neighbor the next day and asked if she had seen anyone, but she had no answers for me. She had heard the pounding, too, but she didn't bother to look out. She thought it had been someone coming to visit me.

When He Knocks

RB: My Aunt Amy, my mother's oldest sister, was one of the best storytellers I ever heard, especially when it came to ghost tales. Her husband, Elmer, died young, leaving Amy with four young children to raise alone. One child died soon after Uncle Elmer, which caused Amy to feel a close connection with those who had passed on. She loved to tell stories of the strange experiences she and Uncle Elmer had had together because they made her a believer in life after death.

Amy would often ride the bus with her children from Cincinnati to Russell Springs to visit us at Christmas. I could hardly wait to hear her stories. Outside, the snow covered the fields and trees like white sheets, giving the illusion that the dead were sleeping peacefully underneath. But inside, the fire crackled merrily and the lamplight pushed the shadows away to the corners of the room. We would all gather close to Aunt Amy as she began her stories. We never questioned a word she said, and I have always assumed they were true.

One of the scariest stories I remember was the experience she and Uncle Elmer had just after they were married. Uncle Elmer took her to his parents' home in northern Kentucky for their first Christmas together. It was not the house where Uncle Elmer grew up, but rather one his parents had purchased at a bargain price later in life.

Amy and Elmer arrived on Christmas Eve, just ahead of a fierce snowstorm that brought with it blizzardlike conditions. Her in-laws' house was much grander than Amy had thought it would be. It had a long porch running the length of the house in front. There were two doors leading onto the porch. As they entered through the one on the right, Amy noticed that the other door had bars across it. That struck her as a bit odd, but she thought maybe it had been a children's playroom and the parents had wanted to make sure the children couldn't open the door and wander outside alone. She dismissed these thoughts from her mind when she saw the beautiful Christmas tree in the living room and smelled the delicious smells coming from the kitchen. With such a wonderful family and surroundings, Amy was delighted that they were going to have a white Christmas. The snowstorm was the perfect touch.

When Elmer started toward the large front room off the living room with the luggage, his mother spoke up quickly.

"I've fixed a room for you upstairs," she said. "You'll be more comfortable up there."

"It's too cold up there, Mom," Elmer said. "We'll use this room with the fireplace."

"But it's snowing tonight," Elmer's mother said. "We do not use this room when it snows."

"That's nonsense," he said quietly. "I don't believe that old tale. We'll be fine."

"What tale?" asked Amy. "What are you talking about?"

"I'm afraid we have a Christmas ghost," Elmer's mother

166

told her. "It came with the house. We don't want it to disturb you."

"A ghost!" exclaimed Amy. "Elmer, you didn't tell me about a ghost!"

"It's just a silly tale," said Elmer. "Some limbs or something just blew against the house, and people got the tale going. It's nothing to worry about. It's a great room with a fireplace. It will be warmer and more cozy than the room upstairs."

Elmer entered the room and put the luggage down. Amy unpacked while her husband got a fire going in the fireplace. She had to admit, it *was* a great room.

Elmer's mother said nothing else about her son's choice of room, but she looked worried all through dinner. By bedtime, the wind was howling fiercely and swirling the snow into a sea of white waves across the yard.

As Elmer's parents started up to bed, his father turned and pointed toward the front room.

"The door has been reinforced and the deadbolts are in place," he said to Elmer. "I hope you both have a good night."

"What did he mean by that?" Amy asked, as Elmer followed her into the room and closed the door behind them. "I'm beginning to get nervous."

"It's nothing to worry about," said Elmer. "Dad just takes precautions when it snows."

"Why?" asked Amy. "Does the door blow open easily?"

"It just needs to stay closed," said Elmer. "Now please get in bed. I'm tired from the driving and I want to sleep."

Elmer fell asleep at once, but Amy lay awake, listening to the wind that had by then risen to a steady roar. There was something about it that made her feel uneasy. It wasn't the storm itself. Something was lurking out there in the darkness. She could feel it coming closer. She told herself that she was just imagining things because she was in a new place, but she knew that wasn't true. There was a presence out there in the storm. Amy concentrated on listening to Elmer's even breathing, and soon the warmth of the room and the handmade quilts on the bed made her drowsy. She drifted off to sleep, too.

After Amy had been asleep for some time, she was suddenly awakened to the sound of pounding on the outside door. She sat up in bed, thinking at first that the wind was blowing a tree limb against the house. She quickly realized it couldn't be that, because there was no tree close enough. Besides, the pounding was accompanied now by a muffled, angry voice.

"Let me in!"

Somebody was obviously out in the blizzard and needed assistance. She reached over to shake Elmer, but was surprised to find that he was already awake. She was puzzled that he wasn't responding to the voice.

"Elmer, get up!" Amy said. "Somebody out there needs help!"

"Just be quiet," Elmer responded. "He'll soon go away."

"You can't leave somebody out in this blizzard!" Amy said. "He'll freeze to death!"

"No, he won't," said Elmer. "He already did!"

"What?" exclaimed Amy. "Is that the ghost your mother was talking about?"

The pounding increased until it shook the door on its hinges, and then suddenly it stopped.

Elmer breathed a sigh of relief.

"It's over," he said. "He won't be back tonight. We can get some sleep now."

"I can't sleep until you tell me what this is about," Amy told him.

Elmer then gave in and told her the history of the house.

"Many years ago," he began, "a man on the next farm lived alone with his daughter. He was drunk most of the time, but it was especially bad during Christmas. His daughter had been born on Christmas Eve, but his wife had died in childbirth. He blamed the little girl for his wife's death and beat the child often in a drunken rage.

"One Christmas, he beat the little girl and passed out from his whiskey. Fearing for her life, the little girl ran to this house for help. The owners took her in just as a terrible snowstorm hit. They called the sheriff, but the storm delayed him. Meanwhile, the girl's father woke up and came looking for her. He knocked and pounded on the door, but they wouldn't let him in. Finally he stopped, and the owners assumed he had gone back home. The next morning, they discovered that he had passed out and frozen to death on the porch.

"Since that night, he knocks on this door only if it snows on Christmas Eve. Tonight was one of those nights. Once, an owner opened the door and died from chills and fever soon after facing the angry ghost. Maybe it was a coincidence, but since then, nobody has wanted to find out what might happen if they come face to face with him."

Amy was grateful that the weather cleared for the rest of their visit. After that, she and Elmer only visited his parents during the warm seasons. They never wanted to be there again when the ghost knocked.

A Father's Christmas Tree

RB: Our favorite Christmas stories were those we retold many times because they were filled with love and hope and the true spirit of Christmas. This is the story of a father whose love lived on after death. There is no documented evidence to prove this story is true, but it is one that most of us would like to think really happened.

In the early 1900s, a flu epidemic hit Kentucky hard. It was a form of flu that the doctors had never dealt with before, so it swept through families, sometimes leaving several members of the same family dead at the same time.

By Christmas Eve it had just about burned itself out, but many who had survived were left trying to recover from its weakening effects. In a house in the hills, a mother named Ella, and her little daughter, Maria, were two such survivors. One member of that household had not been so lucky. Maria's father, William, had lost his battle with the deadly disease. On this Christmas Eve, he was sleeping down the road beneath the snow in the little graveyard by Bethlehem

Church. It would be a bleak Christmas for Ella and Maria without him.

To make matters worse, the first major snowstorm of the season had started about noon, and by dark, blizzardlike conditions were forcing everybody to stay inside.

Maria stood with her nose pressed against the windowpane, watching the snow swirl madly outside. She strained to see beyond the porch, but she could see no star in the sky on this Christmas Eve.

"Come away from the window, Maria," Ella told her daughter. "It's drafty over there. I don't want you getting chilled and taking a backset with the flu."

Maria didn't move. Her eyes remained focused on the swirling snow.

"Maria, come on over by the fire!" her mother said.

"I can't, Momma," Maria answered. "I'm waiting for Daddy to bring our Christmas tree."

Ella blinked back tears. She had explained William's death to Maria, but she obviously didn't understand that he wouldn't be coming home ever again.

"Honey," Ella said, joining her daughter at the window, "you know Daddy can't get us a tree this year. Daddy died and he won't be back. He's in Heaven now."

"Daddy always gets me a tree at Christmas. I know he won't forget. He'll find a way!" Maria insisted.

"Daddy remembered when he was alive, but now he's gone. And I've been too sick to get a tree."

"We have to have a tree," declared Maria. "How will Santa find me if there is no tree in the window?"

"I don't think Santa will be out on a night like this," Ella tried to explain. "He will come when the weather gets better."

"He'll come tonight," said Maria. "Santa likes snow! He'll want us to have our presents on Christmas morning."

Ella thought of the packages she and William had wrapped and left at the country store. William had planned to pick them up and bring them to the house by Christmas Eve, but the flu had taken him before he had a chance to carry out his plan. Ella hadn't had a chance to get them, either. Maria would just have to understand that Santa got delayed this year.

"Come on to the table," Ella said. "I'm heating up the soup for supper."

The two started to turn from the window when they heard a thud on the porch. A shadowy form appeared in the snow, but was gone in a flash into the world of white.

"Momma, somebody put something on our porch! It's a tree, Momma! Daddy brought us a tree!" cried Maria.

While Ella stood staring, not believing what she had just seen, Maria pulled the door open and ran onto the porch.

"Come back!" Ella called to her daughter. "You'll catch your death of cold!"

Maria already had hold of the tree and was trying to drag it inside. Ella dashed to her side and, together, they pulled the tree inside and closed the door. Ella brushed the snow from their shoulders and hair, and wrapped herself and Maria in warm robes.

"I told you Daddy would bring us a tree," said Maria, smiling at her mother.

"Honey, the wind just blew a tree down and it landed on the porch," explained Ella. "It wasn't your daddy!"

"This tree didn't break," Maria pointed out. "It's been cut. There are no jagged edges."

Ella looked and saw that the tree had indeed been cut, just as Maria had said. She searched her mind for a logical explanation.

"A neighbor must have cut the tree and brought it to us," said Ella. "We'll find out later who it was and thank him."

"Momma, I know it was Daddy. Didn't you see him there before he vanished in the snow?" asked Maria.

Ella had to admit she had seen something, but she wasn't sure what it was.

"Momma, I know Daddy is dead," Maria continued. "But don't you remember the story Daddy used to tell me? He said that Christmas Eve was a special time when animals can talk and the dead are free to walk the earth without leaving any tracks. There were no tracks in the snow when we pulled the tree inside."

"The way the wind is blowing, the snow would have covered any tracks by the time they were made," said Ella.

Maria wasn't listening. She had turned her attention to the tree.

"Momma, can we decorate it?" she asked.

"Okay," Ella agreed, "but let's have our soup first."

She heated the soup and the two sat silently at the table. They both ate hurriedly because the hot soup filled them with warmth and strength.

"Where's the tree stand?" Maria asked as soon as she finished eating.

"It's in the front closet with the ornaments and lights," Ella answered.

Ella cleared the bowls from the table as Maria ran to the closet and opened the door.

"Momma, come quick!" she called. "Look at this!"

Ella ran to the closet.

"Look, Momma! Look at Daddy's shoes! He was here!" said Maria, pointing to the closet floor.

Ella looked down and saw William's shoes, exactly where he left them before he died. But tonight, they were covered with snow.

Maria grabbed the tree stand and rushed to the tree, leaving Ella to bring the box filled with ornaments. When she pulled out the box, she saw what Maria had not seen. There, hidden behind the box, was a stack of packages that they had left earlier at the country store. Ella smiled as she closed the closet door. Maria would have her gifts on Christmas morning after all. On the magical night of Christmas Eve, Ella realized that Maria had been right. The dead could walk the earth! William was with them in spirit. They would never be alone.

Chime Child

RB: There are many magical stories about Christmas, but we don't hear much about chime children today. Dickens wrote about them, though, and oral stories trickled down to us in Appalachia. A chime child is one born when the clock is chiming the magical hours of three, six, nine, or twelve. These chime children are said to have special powers, especially over animals. They are also gifted with knowledge of herbs and healing. Those born at the stroke of midnight are said to be able to see and talk to ghosts.

Erin Blair was such a child. She was born on Christmas Eve, just as the clock chimed twelve to welcome Christmas Day. In her eight years, she had talked to friends that her mother couldn't see, but her mother assumed that Erin was talking to imaginary friends that all children have.

Ever since her father had died in a mining accident, Erin and her mother had lived alone. Her mother took in sewing, raised a garden, and canned food for winter, but it was never enough. She was relieved one day to receive a letter from her grandfather asking them to come live with him and help him out on his little farm.

Erin loved her great grandfather and liked life on the farm, but it was isolated, and there were no children for her to play with.

"Great Grandfather, do you know any children nearby?" Erin asked one day. "I saw a girl in a red coat by the road near the woods the other day."

"You must have been mistaken," he told her.

Erin said nothing more to him, but she knew what she saw.

As Christmas grew closer, Erin would walk in the

woods, looking for pinecones for Christmas wreaths. She saw the little girl in the red coat helping a lady gather herbs near the creek. They waved to each other. Erin picked up some cones, and when she looked again, the lady and child were gone. Erin didn't mention them to her mother and great grandfather. Maybe later, she thought, she would see if she could find their house.

The week before Christmas, it began to snow. Great Grandfather and Erin carried wood into the house from the woodpile in the shed. Erin's mother began baking Christmas cakes and cookies. Great Grandfather cut a Christmas tree and hauled it home.

Then Great Grandfather and Erin's mother announced one morning that they were making a quick trip into town for Christmas surprises.

"Erin," her mother said, "I want you to stay here and make decorations for the tree. Don't leave the house until we get home."

Erin promised, and the time flew by as she made paper chains and stars from paper, glue, and glitter. The wind blew hard and the snow piled up. Erin was getting worried by the time her mother and great grandfather returned. Both were wet and cold. They explained that they were so late getting back because a rabbit had spooked the horse, and the horse had turned the sled over in a snowdrift before they could calm him down. They changed into dry clothes and ate supper, but by morning both were coughing. By late afternoon, both had a high fever and had taken to their beds.

Erin was frightened. She heated some soup, but the little girl didn't know how to care for two people who were so sick. Christmas was only two days away, and it looked like it would be a bleak one. She thought of going for help, but the snow was falling hard and fast now and had already covered the roads. She would never be able to get to town by herself. The two people she loved most were probably going to die and she couldn't help them. Tears were running down her cheeks when she heard a knock at the door.

Erin brushed away her tears and rushed to open the door. There stood the little girl in the red coat, only now it was partially covered with snow.

"Hello!" said Erin. "Come in!"

"I can't," she said. "Momma told me to hurry. She said to tell you to boil these herbs and make a tea. It will make your great grandfather and your mother get well."

The girl handed Erin a bag of herbs and turned to go.

"Thank you!" said Erin, wondering how the girl and her mother knew the two were ill.

The girl nodded and smiled as she walked away.

"Wait! Who are you? What's your momma's name?" called Erin.

"I'm Annie," she called back. "My momma is Molly Weaver."

Then she disappeared into the swirling snow.

Erin hurried to the kitchen and boiled the herbs. She coaxed her mom and great grandfather into drinking some. Later, they were more alert and drank some more. The grown-ups felt cool to the touch now, so Erin figured the fever broke when they drank the tea. The three slept peacefully through the night.

When Erin woke on Christmas Eve, her mother and great grandfather were already up. Both were weak, but the worst was over. Erin knew they would be all right now. Her mother made breakfast, and the three sat down to eat.

"Erin, what is this in the kettle?" she asked. "What did you give us to drink?"

"I don't know," Erin said. "Annie brought it to me. She said her momma said it would make you well."

"Who's Annie?" her mother asked.

"You know. The little girl I saw in the red coat," said Erin.

"I thought you just thought you saw her," her mother said. "There's nobody like that around here, is there, Grandfather?"

The old man's face had grown pale.

"There used to be," he said. "Molly Weaver was a healer. She and her little girl, Annie, were gathering bark near the creek about five years ago. It was snowing and the ground was slippery. They lost their footing and fell into the creek. They both froze to death. Annie was wearing a red coat when they found her."

"I don't understand," said Erin's mother.

"Erin is a chime child," the old man reminded her. "She has the gift. She can see and talk to ghosts. That saved our lives."

A Doll for Christmas

RB: Little Wilma Hopkins wanted a doll for Christmas. She looked through catalogs and pointed out the ones she liked to her mother.

"Honey, we don't have the money to buy a doll for you this Christmas," her mother told her. "We had to use what we got from the tobacco crop to pay taxes. Maybe we can get you one next year."

"Momma, why can't you make me one?" asked Wilma.

"We'll see if I have time," her mother answered. "I have a lot to do before Christmas."

"I know I'll get my doll," said Wilma. "I'll wish really hard."

They didn't say any more about it until the morning of Christmas Eve. Wilma's mother found some scraps of material, and buttons for eyes, but she couldn't find any cotton for stuffing. She remembered she might have some in a bag in the attic.

"Wilma, go up to the attic and see if you can find that old bag of cotton I used to have. It would make good stuffing for the doll."

Wilma hurried to the attic and was gone only a couple of minutes when her mother heard her squeal out in delight.

"Oh, Momma! I found it! I found it!" she called. "It's beautiful! Thank you!"

Mrs. Hopkins got up and walked to the bottom of the stairs as Wilma ran down carrying a beautiful rag doll.

"You sent me up to find it, didn't you?" Wilma exclaimed, still excited. "It's the most beautiful doll I've ever seen!"

"Where did you find that?" Mrs. Hopkins asked. "I didn't make it!"

"But, Momma, it was in the attic waiting for me," said Wilma. "May I keep it, please?"

"Let me see it," Mrs. Hopkins said. "I can't imagine how it got in the attic."

When she took the doll from Wilma's hand, she had the strangest feeling that something was terribly wrong with the doll. She inspected it carefully, but found nothing out of the ordinary. It was odd, but she had a feeling of dread and sorrow when she held the doll.

"I don't know what it is, but there is something about this doll that I don't like," she said. "Exactly where did you find it?"

"It was under the eave by the window near the bag of cotton," Wilma answered.

Mrs. Hopkins couldn't imagine where it came from. Of course, they hadn't lived in this house very long, and there had been some old boxes in the attic when they moved in. She hadn't had a chance to go through them yet. Maybe the doll had fallen out of one of the boxes.

"Momma, may I please keep the doll?" Wilma pleaded.

Other than the uneasy feeling she had, Mrs. Hopkins couldn't think of any reason to say no. She nodded her assent. Wilma hugged her, took the doll, and ran into her room to play.

Mrs. Hopkins went to the kitchen and began preparing dinner, and started thinking about what she could fix ahead of time for dinner on Christmas Day. Her in-laws were coming to eat with them and she wanted to be ready. As she worked, she heard voices in Wilma's room.

That was odd. Wilma never talked to imaginary friends, and Mrs. Hopkins had not heard anyone enter the house.

"Wilma, who's with you?" she called.

"Melissa," Wilma called back.

She must have named the doll Melissa, thought Mrs. Hopkins.

She continued to cook and soon realized that the voices had stopped.

"Wilma," she called, "are you all right?"

There was no answer. That was unlike Wilma. Mrs. Hopkins decided to go check on her. She was shocked to find Wilma lying on the floor with the doll across her nose and mouth. She snatched it off and checked Wilma's pulse. It was steady.

"Wilma, wake up! Wake up!" she said.

Wilma opened her eyes and looked at her mother. She started to cry.

"The doll's mean, Momma! Melissa came to take the doll back, but it wanted me to go, too. They pushed me and I fell. Then everything went black."

Mrs. Hopkins held her while she sobbed quietly.

"It's okay, honey," she told her. "It's okay."

Mrs. Hopkins looked at the doll. Its features had

changed. Its eyes were staring at her, and the grin on its face was pure evil.

"Come on, Wilma," her mother said. "We're going to get rid of that doll!"

Mrs. Hopkins picked up the doll, carried it to the living room, and threw it in the fireplace. It popped and cracked as it burned, and the smoke, swirling and black, went up the chimney.

"Who was Melissa?" Mrs. Hopkins asked Wilma.

"I don't know," said Wilma. "She said she lived in the attic."

Mrs. Hopkins didn't press Wilma for more details. Mr. Hopkins had nothing to add about the mysterious doll when he came home that night. He had never seen it in the attic, but agreed with his wife that she was right to destroy it. That night, after everyone else was in bed, Mrs. Hopkins worked way into the night and made Wilma a new doll.

The next morning, Wilma was delighted with her new doll. She seemed to have no ill effects from the ordeal she had gone through on Christmas Eve.

Mrs. Hopkins had dinner almost ready when her in-laws arrived. While her husband took his father out to look at the barn, Mrs. Hopkins and her mother-in-law started putting food on the table. They talked as they worked, and she told her mother-in-law about the incident with the doll.

"Oh, my!" her mother-in-law said, putting her hand over her heart and sitting in the nearest chair. "I wondered if you would have any weird experiences when you moved here. I have heard all my life that a witch lived here many years ago and kept her daughter locked in the attic. She put a spell on her daughter's doll so the doll would keep other children away. I figured it was just a story, even though people swore it was true. You did the right thing to burn that doll!"

"What were their names?" Mrs. Hopkins asked.

"The woman was just called Witch Woman," she said, "but the little girl's name was Melissa."

The Ghost That Hated Christmas

RB: For many people, Christmas is the best time of the year. It is hard to imagine anyone but Scrooge hating Christmas, but one story we heard as children told of a ghost who hated Christmas, too.

Old June Miller was a witch. The name "June" didn't fit her at all. She was not warm, and life around her was not rosy. Mean frowns had left lines in June Miller's face, and harsh words had made her voice hoarse and croaky. Her eyes reflected the darkness of the stormiest summer night, and her heart was as cold as a bitter January day.

June had several acres of land near Damron's Creek, and lots of pine and holly trees grew near its banks. Everybody eyed the pine and holly trees as Christmas grew near because they wanted to cut them down for decorations. Old June would have none of that, and she guarded her property with her shotgun. More than one would-be thief had felt the sting of buckshot when they tried to sneak on her land and get by her.

Old June didn't participate in any holiday traditions.

When the church choir went from house to house caroling, she drove them away. And when the kind ladies of the neighborhood came bearing gifts of cookies and cakes at Christmas, she refused to let them come in. Once she screamed at Pastor Boyd when he invited her to help decorate the tree for the Christmas party at church.

"I hate Christmas!" she'd yell. "It's all nonsense. I want no part of it, so leave me alone!"

A few older citizens in the community remembered that June had once had a husband and son, but they had died in a fire started by defective Christmas lights. She had hired neighbors to tear down the remains of her old house and build another one for her near the creek. She moved into the new house and never celebrated Christmas again.

On her deathbed, June declared, "Nobody will ever celebrate Christmas in this house. I dare them to try!"

She had no heirs except a distant cousin in another state. The cousin sold the property to the McClain family, who had a young son named Leslie. They heard about Old June's dying declaration, but they just considered it the ravings of a sick old woman.

The McClains were well liked in the community, and Leslie became best friends with a young man named Hugh. One night in December, Hugh was visiting the McClains to help decorate the family's Christmas tree. It was their first Christmas in this house, so the McClains were excited. Snow began falling heavily and built up on the roads, so Hugh accepted the McClains' invitation to stay the night. When the tree was finished, the family and their guest got ready for bed. Mrs. McClain made up a bed on the couch for Hugh, and soon they were all settled in for what they thought would be a peaceful night's sleep.

About 4:00 A.M., Hugh was jarred awake by a crash. The storm had ended, and in the moonlight streaming through the window he could see a vase lying smashed on the floor. At that instant, Leslie's cat jumped on Hugh's chest, so he assumed that the cat had knocked over the vase. He set the cat on the floor and turned over to go back to sleep, but the cat let out the most unearthly shriek Hugh had ever heard in his life! Hugh sat up and looked in the direction the cat was looking. Its back was arched, and it was hissing at something in the corner. Hugh could tell something was there, but he couldn't see it clearly. It was a dark form facing the Christmas tree. Suddenly, the ornaments and lights on the tree began exploding like they had been shot!

The noise woke Leslie and his parents, and they came rushing into the room to see what was happening. They stopped in their tracks as the tall Christmas tree toppled over in the floor in front of them. At the same time, a windowpane shattered and a freezing wind swept around the room and out again.

Then the house fell silent. The McClains and Hugh all stared at each other in shock. Then they set about cleaning up the mess. Nobody could go back to sleep, so Mrs. McClain fixed an early breakfast and they all sat around eating and comparing notes about what they had seen. They all came to the same conclusion. Hugh wasn't the only visitor that night. They were all convinced that Old June Miller had come to call.

The Christmas Globe

RB: Miss Ellen lived alone amid the rolling hills of Kentucky. She had been married, but her students all called her Miss Ellen. It had been many years since she had actually worked as a teacher, but the name stuck.

Her nearest neighbors were the Dixons in the valley below her. The distance was close enough for them to see each other's light in the window at night. It was a comfort to Miss Ellen to know she had friends close by.

Miss Ellen's nephew, Wilber, did not like the idea of his aunt living so far away from town. When her husband Riley died, Wilber had tried to get his aunt to move, but she wouldn't hear of it.

"My dear Riley is dead," she said, "but I can feel him beside me here in this house. I might lose that feeling if I moved away. Besides, the Dixons are just a stone's throw away. They'd help me if I needed help."

"What if you got sick?" her nephew persisted. "You don't have any way to get word to me. You really should think about moving."

All his words failed to persuade her. In the end, he had to let his aunt have her way, leaving him only to hope for the best.

Miss Ellen occupied her time at home with reading, sewing, and canning the things she grew in her garden. The

Dixons often invited her to share holiday dinners with them. On one particular Christmas Eve, she had gone to have dinner with the Dixons as usual, taking with her the gifts she had for the family. She had knitted sweaters for Mr. and Mrs. Dixon, and she had purchased two books and a game for little Mark from the Sears and Roebuck catalog.

The Dixons had a gift for Miss Ellen, too. It was wrapped in tissue, and Miss Ellen gasped in delight when she pulled the paper off. It was a Christmas lamp! A tiny tree was etched in the globe and hand-painted green. On the top was a red star. When the lamp was lit, it would look like a Christmas tree decorated in red and green, with yellow light around it.

"Oh, how beautiful! I've never seen one like it!" Miss Ellen exclaimed.

"The artist owns the little gift shop in town," said Mrs. Dixon. "She makes one-of-a-kind gifts, you know. When I saw this lamp, I thought of you. I thought maybe your nephew was right."

"Right about what?" asked Miss Ellen.

"I got to thinking of what he said about your not having any way to let us know if you needed us. When I saw that globe, I knew those Christmas colors would give a different light from your other lamps. You can put it in the window and light it if you need our help," said Mrs. Dixon.

"That's a wonderful idea," said Miss Ellen. "Thank you!"

When Miss Ellen was ready to go home that night, snow and freezing rain had started to fall. Mr. Dixon walked her home and saw her safely inside.

"I'll get you some oil for the lamp when I go to town this week," he promised.

After he left, Miss Ellen placed the lamp on the table in front of her window. She would fill it up when Mr. Dixon brought her the oil.

Miss Ellen put on her flannel gown and house slippers and headed for bed. As she passed the stove, she saw that she hadn't brought in a load of wood from the back porch to start a fire the next morning. She opened the door and stepped out to get the wood. She gave no thought to the snow and freezing rain that had left an icy glaze on the front of the porch. She did not think of the slick-bottomed slippers she had just put on. Before she knew it, she was sliding toward the edge of the porch and losing her balance.

Oh, Riley, what a foolish thing I've done, she thought.

As she fell, she thought she heard Riley's voice.

"It's okay, Ellen. You'll be okay."

Then she hit the snowy ground and the white world went black.

She woke up in bed with anxious faces staring at her. The Dixons and Doc Lawrence were there.

"'Bout time you came around," the Doc said.

"What happened?" asked Miss Ellen. "I just remember falling."

"You weren't hurt much. It just knocked the wind out of you. But you would have frozen to death if the Dixons hadn't found you," said Doc Lawrence. "I'll be going now. The Dixons are going to stay with you. I'll check back tomorrow."

She thanked the doctor, and he left. Then she looked at her friends.

"How did you know I fell?" she asked.

"I saw the Christmas globe in the window," said Mr. Dixon. "I had just started in the door at home, when something made me look back. There were the Christmas lights, bright red and green, shining from that globe. We thought we'd better come over to make sure you were all right."

"How did you get oil in the lamp so fast?" asked little Mark. "And how did you light the lamp if you had fallen in the snow?"

"Yes, I want to know how you did that, too," said Mrs. Dixon.

"I didn't do it," said Miss Ellen. "I didn't have any oil. And I didn't light the lamp. I am sure Riley did! As I fell, I heard his voice telling me I would be okay."

"But Mr. Riley's dead, Miss Ellen!" said Mark. "How could he be here?"

"Why, child," she answered, "don't you know that on Christmas Eve, the dead are free to walk the earth? I know he was with me, and he made the light of love shine in that window tonight."

A Mule's Christmas Eve

RB: My grandmother Alley had special healing powers. She collected herbs and knew how to use them to cure lots of illnesses. She was also a midwife, bringing quite a few babies into the world. When a doctor was not available, people sent for my grandmother. It wasn't until one cold Christmas Eve that we learned she had special powers over animals, too.

It is said that on Christmas Eve, animals have the power to talk and to understand what people say. Grandmother Alley believed this to be true, and she put it to the test.

One Christmas Eve when my grandparents' children were small, Grandfather Alley took the wagon and the team of horses and went to the little country store to get some gifts and Christmas goodies. Grandmother Alley was home cooking supper and trying to keep her children busy until it was time to eat. They were just getting over the flu, and she wanted them to play games quietly and rest.

A freezing rain had set in right after dark, and Grandmother Alley was hoping Grandfather wouldn't stay long at the store. Sometimes he stayed and talked a while. She liked to have her family in by the fire on cold winter nights.

Her beans were done and she had just taken the cornbread from the oven when she heard a horse approaching. Then she heard a knock on the door. She opened it, and there stood little Ray Foley. She was surprised to see him out on a night like this because he was getting over the flu like her own children.

"Lord, child!" she said. "Come in! You're going to catch your death of cold out in the rain!"

"Momma sent me to get you," he gasped. "She says the baby's coming now!"

"Where's your daddy?" Grandmother asked.

"He went to get the doctor," Ray answered, "but you know how Doc is. He's always off somewhere when you need him. Momma's afraid they won't get back in time. She needs you! Please hurry!"

Grandmother had a problem. Grandfather had the wagon and the horses, and he had gone in the opposite direction from the Foley place. She didn't know for sure when he'd get home. Her only other means of transportation was the buggy and Old John, their stubborn old mule, and Old John didn't like going anywhere in the rain.

"Momma told me to hurry back," said Ray. "Will you come on over right away?"

Grandmother Alley made her decision. She'd have to hitch Old John to the buggy and go.

"You go on home and tell your mother I'll be right there," she said. "Don't worry. I'll be right behind you."

Ray mounted his horse and rode off into the rainy night. Grandmother told the children where she was going.

"The beans and bread are on the table, so go ahead and eat your supper. Your daddy should be home soon. I want you to stay in by the fire and tell him where I am when he comes. I may be with Mrs. Foley all night."

She put on her coat and hat and grabbed a lantern and her bag of herbs. At the barn, she quickly hitched Old John to the buggy. She hung the lantern on the side of the buggy and climbed in. She placed the bag of herbs behind the seat. Old John balked a bit at first, but finally they were on their way.

Grandmother only used Old John for transportation

when she absolutely had to. Old John had a mind of his own, but there was one thing the family could always count on. He'd always run if the driver dropped the reins. Ever since they'd bought him years before, he had never once failed to run when the reins were dropped. Grandmother held the reins tightly as they moved along the narrow, muddy road.

They were about halfway to Mrs. Foley's house when Grandmother heard a low groan beside the road.

"Whoa, John!" she called out.

For once, Old John actually obeyed. He stopped and stood still. That in itself seemed like a Christmas Eve miracle to Grandmother.

She held tightly to the reins with one hand as she leaned over to see where the groaning had come from. From the lantern light, she could see someone lying off the side of the road in a shallow ditch. Still holding on to the reins, she climbed down from the buggy for a closer look. It was little Ray Foley! His horse was nowhere to be seen. It must have thrown Ray, and the fall knocked him out. Grandmother would have to lift Ray into the buggy, but he was just out of reach if she held on to the reins.

Grandmother Alley had a difficult choice to make. She could leave Ray there and go for help, but he could die if he were left exposed to the freezing rain. Besides, she didn't know which way to go. If she went on to Ray's house, Mr. Foley and the doctor might not be back yet, so there would be no one to come back for Ray. If she went back home, Grandfather might not be back from the store. But if she dropped the reins so she could get to Ray herself, Old John was sure to run. She might not be able to stop him, and then she and Ray would both be stranded in the cold. She looked around, hoping to see someplace to tie him up, but there was no place she could use. Grandmother made her decision.

Holding the reins in her hand, she walked up to Old John and looked him straight in the eye.

"John," she said, "you've got to help me. I have always believed that humans and animals can communicate in a special way on Christmas Eve, so listen to me carefully. I've got to drop the reins and lift Ray into the buggy. You have to be still and let me do it. John, tonight you can't run!"

She thought she saw Old John nod his head, so she took a chance. Slowly, she dropped the reins and stepped to Ray's side. As she lifted him in her arms, she heard the buggy move forward.

Oh, Lord, He's going to run! she thought.

Then she heard the buggy stop. John had pulled the buggy forward so that the seat was right in front of her. She placed Ray on the seat and climbed in the buggy beside him. She picked up the reins, and Old John started to move again, and he didn't stop until they were at the Foley place.

Grandmother Alley brought another little baby boy into the world that Christmas Eve, and she doctored Ray so he did fine. She didn't know if a spirit or angel had been on the road to keep Old John from running, but she was very grateful to that old mule, who seemed to listen and understand what she told him. He got an extra helping of food on Christmas morning.

That was Old John's one good deed, though. After that

night, he went back to his old ways. For the rest of his life, if they dropped his reins, he would always run.

We always thought that Grandmother Alley continued her good deeds after she died. She had a big book of herbs that was left behind when she died and, after she was gone and somebody got sick, we would find that book open at the very herb we needed.

The Starving Ghosts

LB: There is a belief among those who live in the mountains that you should set a place at the table on Christmas Eve when a loved one dies. Because spirits can walk the earth on Christmas Eve, the thinking goes, the dead one can come and share the festive meal with you. According to this story, some ghosts set their own places at the table.

James Mitchell and his family lived in a nice log house on the side of a mountain in the eastern part of Kentucky. It was the Christmas season, and the Mitchells were preparing for the traditional holiday feast. Mrs. Mitchell started baking cookies days in advance, followed by homemade whiskey cakes. James had already provided the turkey, and his wife had brought in vegetables from the cellar out by the smoke-house. On Christmas Eve, the meal was coming together, and the Mitchell children, Nathan and Rebecca, had the table all set and ready.

Snow had been coming down for days, and the surrounding scenery was fit for any picture an artist would want to paint. James cast a worried eye up the mountain as the snow piled up. He hoped it would stop soon.

"Can we eat now, Momma?" asked Nathan. "I'm hungry."

"Me, too!" said Rebecca.

"All right!" laughed Mrs. Mitchell. "Pull your chairs up to the table. It's ready!"

Just as their chairs were all in place, a great rumble started above the cabin.

"What's that?" asked Nathan.

"Avalanche!" James yelled. "Get under the table!"

Before they could move, the snow roared down the mountain, burying the Mitchells inside their house. It was days before help came. There was no great damage to the structure, but the Mitchells were dead by the time rescue crews found them. One beam had fallen across the table and trapped them there. They had died of cold and starvation. They never got to eat their Christmas Eve dinner.

James Mitchell's brother Ivan inherited the big log house. He and his wife, Carrie, repaired it and moved into it in late summer. Things went along fine for a while. Autumn came and went. Then Christmas approached, and Carrie began thinking about the holiday menu. She prepared everything she could in advance. On the night before Christmas Eve, she and Ivan had just gone to bed when they heard a noise in the kitchen.

"What on earth is that?" asked Carrie. "Something's in my pots and pans!"

"It's probably a mouse," Ivan answered.

"A mouse!" cried Carrie. "I'll have you know there are no mice in my house."

The pots and pans rattled louder.

"Maybe somebody's in the house," she suggested.

"Could be," he agreed. "Stay here while I check."

"Be careful!" warned Carrie.

She listened as Ivan entered the kitchen, walked around, and came back to bed.

"Well, what was it?" she asked.

"Nothing," he said. "Nothing was in there."

"Then what made that noise?" Carrie wondered. "Something had to make it! What's wrong?" she asked, when she saw the look on her husband's face.

"Nobody's in the kitchen, Carrie," he said, "but your pots and pans are on the stove like somebody's ready to cook. Are you sure you didn't set them out?"

"Of course I'm sure!" she insisted.

"Well, there's nothing we can do about whoever put them out, so let's get some sleep," said Ivan.

They tried, but neither slept well that night. When daylight finally arrived, they got up. Dishes were rattling in the kitchen, but nobody was there.

"Ivan, I don't want to stay here tonight. Please! It's James and his family; I know it is. Let's go stay with my parents tonight," begged Carrie.

Ivan pretended to agree reluctantly to humor her, but the truth was that he didn't want to stay there either. Carrie's parents lived down the road, so they drove there and explained what happened.

"While the women fix supper, let's drive down and see what we can find," suggested Carrie's father.

He and Ivan drove back to Ivan's house. They didn't want to go inside, so they stood outside the window and looked in. They heard chairs being pulled up to the table. They heard the clink of silverware against china plates. Glasses were rising in the air, but there were no people! The starving ghosts of the Mitchell family were finally getting to eat their holiday meal.

Christmas Guide

RB: A neighbor shared a story with us about something that happened to him years ago.

It was a Christmas Eve during World War II, and I was a young soldier with an unexpected pass from Fort Knox to come home. Home to me was my grandmother's farm in south central Kentucky. She lived with my Uncle Josh and Aunt Clara, who took care of her and ran the farm. They had taken me in and raised me after my parents were killed in a car wreck when I was a boy. I hadn't heard from them all week, and I could hardly wait to get home and surprise them.

From Fort Knox, I took a bus to Louisville. I decided I'd better hitchhike the rest of the way if I wanted to get home that night because buses didn't run often down that way. I got a ride with a trucker all the way into Columbia. A local man gave me a ride up the road that passed within a mile of the farm. The sky had looked threatening when we left

Louisville, but it didn't really start to come down until we reached Greensburg. It was building fast by the time we left Columbia and started up Highway 80.

"We've already had some snow this week," the man told me. "I would drive you all the way to the farm, but the snow has drifted and made some of the country roads impassable. I hate to let you out in a snowstorm, but I can't afford to get stuck off the highway."

"I've walked to the farm before in snowstorms," I told him. "Besides, I dressed for the cold. I'll be fine."

As soon as he let me out and drove away, I knew I had not made a wise decision. The cold was brutal after the comfort of the car, but I told myself the sooner I started walking, the sooner I would be home.

The drifts had indeed covered the road like the man said, and I found it difficult to stay on course. The deep snow fell into my boots, and soon my feet were wet and numb.

I must be halfway there, I thought. *I've got to keep going. Nobody knows I'm out here. I should have let them know.*

I was used to hiking, but I began to feel exhausted. I wanted to sit down and rest for just a minute, but I knew that was a very dangerous thing to do. A log was lying across the road right in front of me, so I brushed off the snow from it and disregarded my warning thoughts. I needed to stop and get my bearings. I couldn't be lost this close to home, but in the snow everything looked unfamiliar. I sat there looking around me and my head nodded forward. It would feel so good to sleep for a little while. As I began to give in to the feeling, I saw a light up ahead on my right. It was Uncle Josh on his sled with a lantern. He was wearing his mackinaw—I would have recognized that anywhere! Uncle Josh always wore it when he was hunting or gathering wood. It was odd I didn't hear him or his horse, but I didn't think much about it.

"Am I glad to see you!" I said as I sat down on the sled behind him.

He didn't answer, and I realized it was not wise to talk into the biting wind. I still felt miserable from the cold, but I knew I was safe now with Uncle Josh to take me home. I didn't know how he knew to meet me, but I figured he was looking for firewood and saw me.

It was getting more difficult to stay awake, but suddenly I saw the light in the window at Grandmother's house. Uncle Josh stopped the horse, and I jumped off the sled and ran to the porch as fast as I could. The door opened as I was stomping my feet to get the snow off my boots. Grandmother was standing there, obviously overcome with emotion at seeing me. She was crying as she put her arms around me and pulled me inside.

"How on earth did you get here?" she asked.

"I hate to admit it," I said, "but I got lost out there. I was getting a little scared when Uncle Josh showed up with the sled."

"What on earth are you saying?" she said. "Who brought you home? Where did he go?"

"I guess he went to put up the horse and sled," I told her. "I jumped off and ran in when he stopped."

She had turned pale now, and her hand was trembling. "Oh, Lord!" she said. "Didn't you get my telegram? Don't you know what happened?"

"I didn't get a telegram," I said. "It must have come after I left. Tell me! What happened?"

"Your Uncle Josh couldn't have been out there in the woods tonight. He was killed in a logging accident yesterday afternoon."

"That can't be! He brought me home! Look at the tracks in the snow!"

I ran to the door and flung it open. Side by side, we stood staring from the house to the woods. The wind had died down. The clouds had broken, and the moon had come out. There was no sign of a horse, sled, or any tracks, even the ones I would have made. The moonlight shone on the pure white snow, undisturbed and unbroken.

The Black Dog

RB: In ghost lore, black dogs are usually signs of trouble. You never want to meet one, but if you do, you must not pass it. If you do, something terrible will happen. My aunt Polly had an encounter with a black dog that saved the life of her and her sister, and she told us this story.

I didn't pay any attention to superstitions like black dogs, but after what happened to my sister Amy and me, I think maybe I should have. In fact, it may be more truth than superstition.

Amy and I had parts in our school's Christmas program, and the teacher called a rehearsal at night. Amy was fourteen and I was ten, and Dad said we could get a ride with our neighbors to the school and then walk home by ourselves. We had grown up a lot from necessity since our mother died three years before, and Dad trusted us to do things on our own.

Our neighbor lived on the main road about a half-mile from our house. We'd had a cold spell, and ice had formed on the big rocks on the high banks on one stretch of the road where we had to walk. The weather had turned warmer lately, so we were fairly comfortable all bundled up in our coats. We arrived at our neighbor's house without incident and rode with them to school.

The rehearsal had some rough spots, so we stayed until everything had been worked out. We were using live animals for the manger scene, and the donkey did not want to cooperate. We were all laughing about it as we rode back with the neighbors to their house. Amy and I got out of the car and headed toward home.

"Are you sure you girls will be okay?" they asked.

"Sure, we'll be fine," we told them.

We had our lantern with us, so we were not afraid.

Our neighbors said goodnight and went inside, and Amy and I started walking down the road. We hadn't gone far when the lantern suddenly went out.

"Did you put oil in this?" Amy asked.

"No, I thought you were going to fill it up," I answered.

"Great!" said Amy. "Now we have to walk home in the dark!"

We were nearing the section of road with the high banks on each side. Shadows filled the roadway, so I hurried to stay close to Amy as we walked through this part.

"It's really dark," I said. "I can't see where to walk."

"Just stay on the road, silly girl," Amy said. "It's not a very long stretch. We'll be through it in no time. Besides, the moon is giving a little light."

I realized she didn't sound as sure of herself as she usually did, so I moved to her side. We were now in the dark shadows between the high banks.

Ahead, something gave a low growl, and we saw two red eyes looking at us! I grabbed Amy's arm and we both took a step back. Slowly from the shadows, a big black dog emerged.

"Whose dog is that?" I asked. "I don't know anybody around here that's got a dog like that!"

"Me, either," said Amy. "Just stand still and maybe it will leave us alone."

I didn't obey—I moved to the right a little. The dog moved, too, and gave another low growl. I stepped quickly back to Amy's side and didn't move again.

"How are we going to get around it?" I asked. "It doesn't want us to pass."

"We're not going to pass it," said Amy. "Look closely. You can see through it. It's a ghost dog!"

"Oh, Lord," I said, almost crying. "How will we get

home? They say something bad will happen if you pass a black ghost dog!"

Just then we heard a rumble from the bank. This was followed at once by a tremendous crash as a huge rock fell from the bank to the road. Dirt and pieces of ice slid onto the road where the rock came to rest.

We held each other tightly as we watched the black dog disappear before our eyes. Everything was silent as if nothing had ever happened.

"We would have been right under that rock slide if the dog hadn't stopped us, wouldn't we?" I asked.

"Yes," said Amy.

"I was so scared, but the dog saved our lives!" I continued.

"I guess people are right about black dogs," said Amy. "Something bad would have happened if we had passed."

We went on home without further incident, but we never forgot our experience. We traveled that road many times after that, but we never saw the dog again or learned where it came from.

Christmas Turbulence

RB: A man told me this story at a paranormal conference. I found it very moving, so I have included it here.

One December day, I was at the Los Angeles International Airport waiting for a delayed flight to take me home to Louisville. A young man sitting beside me in the terminal struck up a conversation. He was waiting to pick up a friend whose flight was also delayed.

"Going home for Christmas?" he asked.

"Yes," I said. "My family lives in Louisville."

His eyes got brighter and his face softened.

"I was in Louisville once," he said. "It's a trip I'll remember as long as I live."

"What happened?" I asked him "Rough weather?"

"A little," he said. "Are you sure you want to hear?"

"Sure," I told him, "if you don't mind talking about it."

"Sometimes it helps to talk," he said. Then he told me this story:

I was flying with my girlfriend, but I'd slept most of the way. I woke with a start as the captain's voice came through the speakers.

"This is your captain speaking. We are now beginning our final approach to the Louisville International Airport. I must ask you to fasten your seat belts and remain seated until we are on the ground. We may experience a little turbulence during our descent with the front that's moved in, but I assure you there is nothing to worry about."

Oh, man! I thought. *Little turbulence and no worry would be a welcome change.* I'd had more than my share of both lately.

I glanced at the vacant seat beside me. I knew Marie was somewhere on the plane, but I knew I couldn't go to her now. She would be all right. I had spent almost every waking moment with Marie since we'd met over a year before. I am a paramedic in LA, and I saw her first at the emergency room, when my partner and I were bringing in a victim who was suffering from smoke inhalation from a brush fire. The nurse at the ER was humming a Christmas song, "Beautiful Star of Bethlehem, Shine On."

She smiled at me when we came in.

"I know that song," I told her. "It's like you."

"Then think of me when you hear it," she laughed.

As we were leaving, I heard the head nurse compliment her on her work. This girl had brains *and* beauty! She was too good to be true.

"Why don't you get her number?" my partner asked.

"Why bother?" I asked. "She'd never go out with me."

"You never know until you try," he said.

"Okay," I said. "I'll try."

I walked back to ask for her number, and she smiled and handed me a slip of paper. She had already written it down.

I called the next day, and we were rarely apart after that.

I marveled at the way Marie fit in with everything in LA. Unlike most pretty girls who came to California, she had no desire to become a movie star. She landed a nursing job and was perfectly content. Her nearest thing to a stage performance was singing in church. She dragged me along to the Christmas program, but I didn't offer much resistance. She had a solo, and I wasn't surprised that it was "Beautiful Star of Bethlehem, Shine On."

Christmas came and went, and life was good. I hadn't always had luck with women, but I felt I'd hit the jackpot this time.

In the spring, we transported a patient to the hospital and stopped to talk to Marie for a minute. When we left, my partner looked concerned.

"Take it easy on that girl, Johnny!" he said. "She looked tired. You must be keeping her up too late."

I hadn't noticed it before, but I realized he was right. Marie did look tired, and that was not like her. I decided to keep an eye on her, and as I watched, I became worried.

Marie continued to be tired and began to fall asleep earlier than she used to. She grew pale, and dark circles formed under her eyes. She seemed to be experiencing pain, but she never complained about it.

"Honey, maybe you should let one of the doctors at the hospital take a look at you," I suggested.

"Maybe I should," she agreed. "I'll do it tomorrow."

When I picked her up, she said the doctor ran some tests and she would get the results the day after tomorrow.

"Good," I said. "That's my day off. I'll go with you."

I was surprised that she didn't object. She actually seemed relieved that I was going with her.

We arrived on time to get the results. I waited while they called her back. The wait was a long one. I flipped through every magazine in the waiting room before they called my name.

"Johnny, would you come back with me, please?"

Something in her voice triggered a deep foreboding. As soon as I walked into the doctor's office, I knew something awful was wrong. Marie's eyes were red from crying, but she seemed to be in control now.

"I have cancer, Johnny," she said as soon as I sat down. I could barely detect a quiver in her voice; I knew I had to be strong for her.

The word *cancer* struck fear in my heart, but I tried not to show it. The doctor was surrounding that awful word with other words like *treatments* and *hope*, but I just kept thinking this couldn't be happening!

Then Marie flew into my arms. I held her while we both cried. Finally I asked, "What can we do?"

"Fight it!" the doctor told us.

As his words sank in, I left my youth behind me. I loved this woman, and I had to help her through this.

We fought every step of the way together. So many things were almost too hard to bear: the chemo, the nausea, the hair loss, the wig, the weight loss, and finally the radiation that made Marie weak and deathly ill, but it was to no avail.

"I want to be buried at home," Marie said. "Johnny, please take me home to Kentucky. I've made all the arrangements."

I promised her, and she died in my arms just as the sun set over the blue Pacific.

Marie's journey had ended, but I had one more to make.

The flight to Kentucky was hard. The hearse was waiting when we landed. I was relieved that Marie had handled the arrangements a few weeks before she died. I felt out of place in rural Kentucky.

The hearse and the driver took us to Marie's family, and when we arrived, they all swarmed around us. The neighbors were there, too. They wanted to meet Marie's guy from California.

"You must be starved, Johnny," Marie's mother said. "Come on in. There's plenty of food inside."

I had never been to an Irish wake before, but I tried to fit in. Everybody ate and laughed and traded stories about Marie. Later, I went with the family to church and sat in the front row with them. I listened to the service, but it seemed unreal. Soon it was time to say good-bye and catch my flight home.

I looked at Marie in her coffin. I leaned over and kissed her brow. My eyes filled with tears as I turned and walked to the car that was waiting to take me back to Louisville International Airport. I didn't look back. I knew it would hurt too much to leave her.

The car sped through the darkening countryside to the lights of the airport. I boarded the plane and found my seat. The plane gathered speed, lifted off the runway, climbed and banked, and headed west through a clear night sky. I saw one star brighter than the others and I thought of Marie and her favorite song. I thought of LA and of my partner, who would be waiting at the airport to pick me up.

My eyelids drooped, heavy with exhaustion from the emotions of the day. I was asleep by the time the plane was in straight and level flight. There was no turbulence now.

My partner was waiting for me when the plane landed in LA and he drove me home. "Do you want me to stay a while?" he asked.

"No, thanks," I told him. "I'm going to shower and go straight to bed. It's a workday tomorrow."

"The Captain said to take all the time you need," my partner reminded me.

"I'll do better at work," I said. "I want to keep busy."

I welcomed the long work hours in the days to come. I couldn't believe Marie was gone. I focused on my work and tried to shut out the pain. As the Christmas season approached, my heartache was almost unbearable.

My partner and the other guys I worked with tried to distract me. We had dinner. We went bowling. I even shopped for my partner's two children, but I couldn't help thinking of how happy things had been just one year ago. Now Marie was buried in the Kentucky bluegrass that she had loved, and I was here in LA. We would never be together again. It was so unfair! I began to question the faith that I once held dear.

I volunteered to work on Christmas Eve. I had no family, so I had no reason to stay home. Let the guys with families have the time off.

The night started off slowly. Then we had several runs, one after the other. At about 3:00 A.M., we were called to a fire in an old apartment building. The people had been rescued, but the flames were raging and driving the firefighters back. My partner for the night and I were putting on our gear when a woman ran to us, crying hysterically.

"My little boy is in there," she sobbed. "He ran back to get his dog, and they won't let me go after him. Please! You've got to get him out!"

Things happened fast at that point. The chief ordered us in as a police officer pulled the woman back.

"Take one look and get out fast!" the chief told us.

The apartment was on the first floor, but we still had precious little time. We found the boy and his dog on the floor near the door, and we grabbed them and started to leave. As we turned to make our exit, part of the ceiling came crashing down. The way we had come in was blocked, and the smoke was so thick that we couldn't see two feet beyond our faces. My partner and I recognized the trouble we were in. We were trapped, and death seemed certain.

That's when I heard it. A voice was singing softly, "Beautiful Star of Bethlehem, Shine On." It was moving away from us. I knew I was to follow. This was no hallucination.

"Come on!" I shouted to my partner. "This way out!"

He didn't question me. I followed the voice, and he followed me. Suddenly there was a door, and the next thing we knew we were outside. Hands were reaching for the boy and the dog. We took off our gear and flopped down on the ground.

"I don't understand," my partner said. "How did you know where that door was? Had you been there before?"

"No," I said. "I just followed the singing. Didn't you hear it?"

"Singing?" he said. "Are you crazy? I didn't hear anything but that crackling inferno! I thought our number was up."

I smiled as I looked up. I could see one bright star twinkling high above the smoke and the dying flames. I realized that the miles between Kentucky and LA meant nothing. The turbulence of the night left me, and I was at peace. Marie would always be near me in this world until it was time to join her in the next.

Kim's Christmas Spirit

RB: In the early 1990s, a new young teacher named Kim joined the faculty at the school where I was teaching. She worked well with both the students and the faculty, and was soon selected to be our team leader. There was no generation gap with Kim, and no job too big to tackle.

Kim and I both liked to get to school early to get ready for the day. I'd make coffee, and she'd bring bagels to my classroom where we'd do our work and talk. I loved to hear about her family. She and her husband were the parents of a beautiful little girl named Sarah. I looked forward to a "Sarah story" from her each morning.

In late January, Kim began to complain of being tired. This was very unusual for her because she had never been sick a day in her life. Teachers are used to being tired, though, so we all dismissed it as a professional hazard.

One morning in February, she came to my room and sat down as usual, but she didn't have a "Sarah story" that day.

"I don't want you to worry," she said, "but I've got to be out of school for a few days."

I immediately thought something must be wrong with Sarah, because Kim never missed school otherwise.

"What's wrong?" I asked.

"You know I've been feeling tired lately," she explained. "Now something has started sticking in my throat, and the doctor wants me to go into the hospital for some tests. It's probably just my tonsils or something simple like that, but he wants to check it out. I'm sure it's nothing serious."

I was suddenly very concerned. She was probably right about it being nothing serious, but I couldn't shake the feeling that things were never going to be the same. It was one of those defining moments when I knew my life was going to change forever, and not for the better. Even this foreboding did not prepare me for what was to come. She entered the hospital and we all waited for the results.

The results were unthinkable. The tests showed that a huge tumor was wrapped around Kim's heart, extending up into her throat. That was what she had felt sticking. She had major surgery immediately, and most of the tumor was removed, but it was found to be malignant. She had to undergo chemo treatments right away.

Her few days off turned into weeks. Kim loved teaching and hated to be away. I mailed her a card and included a letter every day and kept her up to date on what was going on with our team. We ignored the rule of no prayer in school and gathered every morning before our classes to pray for her.

Kim tackled the cancer head-on like she did her work.

"I don't want Sarah to think of me as a sick mom," she said. "I just want my life to be normal again."

Whatever came up, she handled it with dignity and courage. When her hair began to fall out from the chemo, she had her dad come over and shave her head at a family deck party. Later, her daughter, Sarah, would write that a bird swooped down and took some of the hair for its nest.

By the end of the summer, Kim was ready to come back to work. She wore a turban while her hair was growing in. She was determined to do her job in spite of the fact that she would have to undergo a long series of radiation treatments. Our classrooms were across the hall from each other, so I kept an eye on her. She was frail, but she never slacked up on her work.

"Why don't you stay home until you're feeling better?" I asked her.

"You don't understand," she said. "I've told you I want my life to be normal again! I want things to be like they were before the cancer."

The look in Kim's eye made me realize how important it was to her, so I made a silent vow not to treat her like she was sick. As team leader, she was supposed to be the first link in dealing with discipline problems. When some of the teachers worried about her and tried to handle problems without involving her, she got upset. Some felt sorry for her and made a point not to mention cancer in front of her. Kim, however, did not want sympathy. She wanted to carry her weight. I would send her problem students and say, "Okay, Sicko! Just because you've got a little cancer, don't think you're going to get out of work today!" She'd roll her eyes and laugh; she loved being treated normally.

As the radiation treatments progressed, Kim got weaker

and weaker. I once went to check on her in the bathroom and found her lying curled up on the floor, too weak to get up. We urged her to stay home and rest, but she would show up for work anyway. When she found she couldn't make it through the entire day, I and her fellow teachers would take her classes and call her husband to come get her.

Finally, the treatments ended, and Kim went for tests to see if the cancer was completely gone from her body. On the day the results came, she asked her husband to come to school to tell her in person, regardless of whether the news was good or bad.

We were taking our students to lunch when I saw him waiting in the hallway at the bottom of the stairs. I knew as soon as I saw the look on his face that the news wasn't good. I hurried the students around the corner toward the cafeteria as Kim came down the stairs. I looked back as he approached her and put his arms around her. My heart broke as I saw them start walking toward the office.

As soon as I got the students in the cafeteria, I hurried to the main office. Kim and her husband were leaving, and she was fighting back tears.

"We'll take care of your classes," I told her. "Don't worry."

She nodded.

"The cancer is spreading," she said, "but I'm going to fight it!"

With her husband's arm around her, Kim walked out the front door. It was the last time I ever saw her alive.

Her battle now began in earnest, but she didn't want

visitors. We respected Kim's wishes, but I wrote her a letter every day, as I had done before. I kept her updated on the team's activities. Her mother said she waited each morning for the postman to bring my letter. I talked to someone in her family every night and left a report about her condition on the counter in the front office at school every morning.

In early December, she called me.

"I'm going to the hospital for massive treatments. The doctor told me to get my affairs in order before I go," she said.

I was stunned. The words seemed unreal.

"I want you to know how much you have meant to me," Kim continued. "I have appreciated your daily letters and your help at school. You've been a special friend, and I want you to know I love you."

I told her how special she was to me and that I loved her, too. Somehow we got through all that and said good-bye without breaking down and crying, but the tears came when I hung up the phone. I knew it was the last time I would hear her voice.

Kim entered the hospital. I continued to write and call every day to get a report on how she was doing. Her condition was critical in the days before our Christmas break. She was in and out of consciousness.

On the last morning before our vacation started, I was standing outside my classroom door, on hall duty, watching the students go to their lockers. Suddenly, I was shocked to see Kim standing across the hall by the door to her old classroom. She was absolutely radiant. She looked healthy and full of energy like she did before the cancer struck. She was smiling and watching the students as they walked by. I knew then without a doubt that she had died during the night and that she had come to school one last time to say good-bye. None of the students seemed to be aware of her presence, though.

I inched my way to the teacher by the door next to mine and I said, "Kim's here. She's there by her door."

The teacher said, "What? That's impossible!"

"I know she's not really there," I told her. "I think she must have died in the night and has come to say good-bye."

We looked across the hall, but we only got a glimpse of her before several students walked between us. When they moved on, Kim was no longer there.

At that point the bell rang, and we all went into our classrooms. Homeroom and first period were together, so I checked attendance and we settled down to work. Just then, an announcement came over the speakers asking one of our team teachers to come to the main office to take a call. The teacher next door went down and came back crying. The call confirmed what I already knew in my heart. Kim had died during the night, just as I thought. When the students saw the other teacher at the door crying, they asked me if Kim had died. I wish I could have waited for grief counselors, but I couldn't lie to them about what they had already figured out. I told them the truth.

We obviously could not continue with our regular class-work, but I knew we all needed to do something to keep busy.

"Let's all take out our journals and write what we are feeling right now," I suggested to my students.

We were all writing quietly when there was a knock at my door. I opened it to find a student aide from the office standing there with a big gift box, beautifully wrapped.

"What's this?" I asked.

"It's for you," he answered. "It was left in the office to be delivered to you today."

I took the box and read the name aloud. It was from Kim! The students gasped, and then there was total silence. I learned later that Kim had shopped and left gifts for all of us on the team. They were to be delivered the last day before Christmas break—the day she died, as it turned out.

"Open it, Mrs. Brown," one boy said.

I opened the gift and showed the class. It was a hand-painted green wooden Christmas tree, with a red holder for a candle on each branch. There was a little tin box filled with white candles and matches. On the lid were painted chipmunks and raccoons, and the words "Friends Forever." That little box has been on my desk ever since.

Kim was buried on a bleak December day in a little country cemetery nestled among rolling hills where she often went in life. Splashes of festive, seasonal colors that she loved dotted the landscape in the distance, reminding us that the bare branches of surrounding trees would, like Kim, blossom again with new life. I especially knew this was true, for I had been privileged to see her when she came to take that last look around the school she loved just after she had died.

Dillon's Restaurant

LB: All winter ghosts do not appear at Christmas. Some turn up at various winter outings.

On January 26, 2007, our friend Robert Parker, Roberta, and I ate one final dinner at Dillon's Restaurant at 2001 South Hurstbourne Parkway in Louisville before it closed its doors for the last time.

Roberta and I arrived first, so we waited in our car for Robert. We looked at the interesting old building while we waited, and as we did we noticed a man looking out at us from a window at the top. We had heard that the owner's demand for higher rent and extensive remodeling was forcing the restaurant to close, so we assumed a man was up there packing things to move away.

When Robert arrived, the three of us took time to study the restaurant, which had been built onto the back of the Funk farmhouse about fifteen years earlier. We learned from a plaque displayed on the front porch by the door that the house was originally known as Avon. The Funk family built the house in 1784. The house changed ownership from the Funks to the Zehenders, who sold it to the Quinn family in 1842. The Quinns named the property Cherry Springs. Cherry Springs is believed to be the second oldest home in Jefferson County, Kentucky. The last of the Quinns sold the property in the early 1900s and it became Dillon's Restaurant.

Jude, the manager of the restaurant, and his mother, Wilma, who was acting as hostess, graciously gave us a tour of the building. We were pleased that they were also willing to tell us about the ghostly experiences that had taken place there through the years. Late-night custodians were hassled by unseen companions, who would move silverware and drop it on the floor. When the moon was just right, other workers sometimes saw images of Civil War soldiers at the bar. Once when the late night manager was on duty, the restaurant was robbed. The manager felt something like a hand pressing on his shoulder as the robbery was in progress, keeping him calm and safe through the entire ordeal.

"I guess the scariest thing happened to a teenage employee late one night here in the restaurant," said Jude. "He was getting ready to leave for the night when a white, misty cloud surrounded him. By the time he reached home, he became so cold and ill that he had to go to the hospital. His condition and recovery were mysteries to the doctors. They had started an IV and were monitoring his heart when suddenly his vitals returned to normal."

"Did you see him again?" I asked.

"Yes," Jude answered, "but he didn't return to work here, though. He went on to become a firefighter. The other firefighters at his station often come to the restaurant, but the young man has never set foot in here again. He said he never wanted to encounter that unearthly white mist again."

We were spellbound by the stories, but a little disappointed that we did not experience anything unusual ourselves. We asked Jude if he'd had any experiences of his own. He admitted that sometimes he felt like he was being watched.

That reminded me of the man we had seen at the window while we were waiting for Robert.

"I know what you mean," I said. "A man was watching us from that top window when we first got here. It was kind of spooky, even though we figured he was up there packing."

"That's strange," Jude said. "That window was put in for decoration. It's a false window. There's no room behind it. Nobody could be up there!"

Was a ghost there taking one last look at the place, as we were doing?

Sadly, the restaurant closed as scheduled the next day. Another business is there now. When I drive by, I wonder if the ghosts stayed behind in the building to watch different customers come and go.

The Poet's House, a Bed-and-Breakfast

LB: On Friday, February 23, 2007, Roberta and I went with two friends, Robert Parker and Sharon Brown, for a relaxing getaway at a bed-and-breakfast called The Poet's House in Ghent, Kentucky. We were delighted to find that it was haunted.

We arrived after dinner, so the owners, David and Rick, offered us refreshments and told us wonderful stories about their unusual experiences in the house. They purchased the Federal-style brick house, with walls "three brick" thick, in March 2005. After renovations were completed, they opened for business in September 2005.

David likes to sit on the couch in the parlor and read. There he has a good view of the hallway. Sometimes he sees shadows go by the door, and their dog, Quinn, often sees the shadows, too. In fact, while David was telling us this story, Quinn suddenly turned his head and looked toward the doorway.

"Look at him," said Sharon. "He saw something just then."

Rick informed us that other guests had heard strange sounds and had seen things in the house, too. They didn't give us the details until later. They wanted us to be open-minded if we saw or heard anything. They only gave us a tour of the house and historical background information.

David and Rick named their bed-and-breakfast The Poet's House after James Tandy Ellis, the most famous resident of the town. Built in 1863, the house is now listed on the Kentucky and the National Registers of Historic Homes.

Ellis was a soldier, politician, musician, author, and poet. He earned national recognition for his newspaper column, "Tang of the South." He also served as Adjutant General of Kentucky. He was a big man, weighing over 300 pounds, and spent most of his time near the end of his life in his bedroom, upstairs from the main floor. He died in his house in 1942 at the age of seventy-four.

James's wife, Harriet, had her own room on the same floor as James's room. She spent many hours by her window, which overlooks the river, watching the river traffic. She became depressed after her husband's death and committed suicide in the house. One obituary says she shot herself in the living room. Another says she shot herself upstairs in her bedroom by her dressing table.

James and Harriet had two children: a boy, who died in infancy; and a girl, who died at the age of five.

After hearing the story of the Ellises, looking at some photographs, and reading some newspaper clippings, the four of us picked our rooms and retired for the night. Sharon chose to stay in the River Dance Cottage next door. Robert took James's bedroom, which has the original bed James slept in. Roberta and I selected Harriet's room, which is considered the most likely suicide site. It was a charming, comfortable room, with one window facing the front street and another facing the river.

At breakfast the next morning, we met eagerly to discuss our experiences of the night before. Rick and David joined us to hear what happened. They told us then of some unexplained noises heard by other guests. They were eager to see if something similar had happened to us.

Sharon, who had stayed in a room on the ground floor, had experienced nothing unusual. The only disturbance she had to report was one she had heard between two small animals under her window.

Robert, however, who had been staying in James Ellis's room, had had some unusual experiences. Right after going to bed, he heard a noise like marbles rolling on the floor in the corner. Immediately after that, he caught a glimpse of a little girl wearing a ribbon and old-fashioned clothes. She looked to be about the age of the Ellis's deceased daughter. Still startled from that apparition, Robert next felt a heavy weight on his bed. He remembered that James had weighed more than 300 pounds and had slept in that bed. The weight remained until Robert started reciting the Twenty-third Psalm; then it vanished.

Roberta and I had a story to share as well. At about 2:00 A.M., we both woke to what sounded like someone walking the perimeter of our bed. It was a tapping sound, like a cane against a wooden floor. Then it would sound like the tapping was in the air, level with the bed. Then something unseen got in bed between us, making a crunching sound, like paper being crumpled. It stayed only a short time and then moved on. Neither of us felt threatened by it. It felt as though someone or something was checking us out.

The night was uneventful after that for Roberta and me, except for the normal street noises of traffic going by out front. But then, around 7:00 A.M., the tapping noise started again. It moved around the three sides of the bed, but never went near the headboard. Maybe it wanted to take a second look at us in the morning light.

After listening to our stories, David and Rick confirmed that other guests had experienced the same strange noises in Harriet's room. They also confirmed that one of the ghosts sighted by other guests has been that of a little girl. Their description of the little girl's old-fashioned clothes and hair ribbon matched the description Robert had just given. The Ellis girl had been buried with her mother's family in Lexington, Kentucky, but perhaps she is lonely and likes to come back home. David and Rick do not know the burial place of the infant son.

The Magnolia House

LB: On December 6, 2006, Roberta was hired to do a storytelling program in Columbia, Kentucky, at the Adair County Middle School. Since we have relatives and friends in that area, I went along to combine work and visits. Tammy, our friend and our contact at the school, arranged for us to stay at the Magnolia House, a bed-and-breakfast in Columbia.

We arrived in town early in the afternoon and went first to the Magnolia House to check in and leave our luggage. Owner Carson Lewis greeted us; his wife and co-owner, Linda, was still teaching in school. He told us we would be the only guests there that night.

When he finished showing us around, Roberta said, "This place would be perfect if you just had a ghost."

To our surprise, Carson smiled and answered, "Actually, we do!"

Of course, we then had to hear all the details.

"On Halloween," said Carson, "someone rings the front doorbell. When we answer, there's nobody there. Naturally, since it happens on Halloween, we thought at first that it was someone playing a prank. We decided to stand by the door and catch the culprit. Well, that didn't work. The bell still rings, even when we are standing there watching. There is nobody anywhere in sight. There is no short in the wiring. And, anyway, it would be quite a coincidence to have a bell short out only on Halloween."

"Anything else?" asked Roberta.

"An odd thing happens in one of our rooms upstairs," he told her. "We'll make the bed and know that nobody is in the room when we leave and go downstairs. When we return, there will be an imprint on the bed where someone or something has been sitting."

"Do you know who the ghost might be?" I asked.

"We're not sure," he said. "We think it might be an old man called Stonewall who used to live upstairs before we bought the place. He really liked it here, so he may have come back after he died."

Carson left us to unpack and look around the place. The old house had been restored and was filled with period furniture of the Old South. Our first-floor room was lovely, with a plush carpet and a very large area rug near the bed. The bed was a huge four-poster, and Roberta noticed that the end of the area rug was leaning against one of the large bedposts at the foot of the bed.

"We need to pull that back onto the floor," she said. "I don't want to trip over it if I have to get up tonight."

We pulled it down and then left to visit some friends and family. Late that afternoon we returned to change and get ready for supper. When we unlocked our door and entered the room, we saw that the rug was back up against the same bedpost. We were certain that nobody had been in our room.

Carson had left before we did. How could the rug be back in that position? We were puzzled, but we pulled it down again and left for supper. After we ate, we went back to our room before going to the school to do the evening program. Roberta was gathering some books and CDs to take along when we noticed that the rug was once again leaning on the bedpost!

We pulled it down, went to the school and did the program, and returned to our room at bedtime. There was the rug leaning against the bedpost one more time.

"Let's pull this as far away from the bed as we can," suggested Roberta. "There is no way this area rug could slide back on this carpet by itself!"

It took both of us pulling as hard as we could to move the rug away from the bed, but we pulled it as far away as it could go. The next morning, the rug was once again leaning against the bedpost! At that point, we let it stay there.

At breakfast, we mentioned our moving rug to Carson and Linda, but they had no explanation. They said that other guests had had the same problem in that room, but nobody knew why the rug kept moving.

In the fall of 2008, we again had a job at Adair County Middle School. We booked the same room at the Magnolia House. When Linda and Carson showed us to our room, we were disappointed to see that the area rug was gone.

"What happened to the rug?" asked Roberta.

"We got too many complaints about it," Linda explained. "We rolled it up and put it in the garage."

Doe Run Inn

LB: Another of Roberta's and my favorite places to visit is Doe Run Inn in Brandenburg, Kentucky. Steeped in the beauty and peace of nature and the charm of the past, and displaying a historical marker denoting its significance, the inn is a welcoming place for both the living and the dead. It is located in an area where Indians hunted before and after the white man came. In 1778, Squire Boone (Daniel Boone's brother) and John McKinney discovered the creek there and named it Doe Run because of the many deer seen there.

Doe Run Inn was originally named Stevenson's Mill. The taller part of the building was built between 1780 and 1790. The smaller part was added between 1800 and 1821. Mainly built with hand-hewn timbers and native limestone, each wall is over two feet thick. One of the old records shows a payment to Tom Lincoln, Abraham Lincoln's father, for his work as a stonemason on the newer part of the building.

Through the years, Stevenson's Mill had to compete with seven other mills located on the creek. For lack of profit, the Stevenson's Mill was shut down and turned into a barn. In 1897, W. D. Coleman, owner of one of the nearby mills, bought Stevenson's Mill to use for a different purpose. The sulfur water in the area was considered by many to have healing properties, so Coleman opened it in 1901 as a family summer resort known as Sulfur Wells Hotel. People came from hundreds of miles away to drink the healing water.

Sometime around 1947, the Haycrafts managed the inn

and turned it into a traditional restaurant and hotel, which they named Doe Run Hotel.

Around 1958, the management changed again, this time to Curtis and Lucille Brown, who changed the name to Doe Run Inn. They ran the inn for over twenty-five years before it passed to other members of the family. The owners during our visit were Ken and Cherie Smith Whitman. Cherie, the grand-niece of Lucille Brown, told us that the property had been in her family for six generations.

The inn has three floors of rooms with antique furnishings and facilities for private meetings or parties. The upper floors were remodeled in 1991 to include bathrooms in most rooms, replacing the dormitory-like structure that had been in place for many years. Along with the changes, the inn endured the presence of some resident ghosts.

The owners and staff members were happy to share eerie experiences and strange stories about the inn with us. A cook's cousin once saw a girl in a mirror while she was cleaning. Others have seen an older man in a rocking chair in Room 12, which is considered to be the most haunted room. Maids report that their shoes are sometimes untied as they stand by beds to make them up for guests. Apron strings are untied in the kitchen, and footsteps can be clearly heard in the lobby and upstairs halls. Vent covers and dishes fall from shelves. Blinds fly up and down, and loud bangs are heard.

Guests often complain of children running in the hall when there are no children there. This activity is often near Room 20, which was once a children's playroom.

The stories focus mostly on five ghosts. One ghost is a very young Confederate soldier in his teens who has a strong southern drawl. Two ghosts are children, a brother and sister. The girl's name is believed to be Annabelle. Another is an older man who could be their father. Both children died accidentally. Legend has it that the girl fell from a front third-floor window and that the boy caught his foot in the creek and drowned. Some have seen the ghostly figure of a woman by the creek; they think it might be the mother of the boy, looking for her lost child. Some sources say a teenage boy fell from a window. Could it have been the young Confederate soldier? The owners said that unfortunately there are no records to back up the legends, but the stories passed on by word of mouth are fascinating.

On February 29, 2008, Sharon Brown, Robert Parker, Roberta, and I spent the night at Doe Run Inn. None of us had heard any of these stories. We arrived at the inn just in time to enjoy a delicious meal in the restaurant.

While we were eating, Roberta glanced out the window at the creek behind the dining room. It looked bleak and gray in the late afternoon light. Suddenly Roberta said she'd just had an image of a woman in a white summer dress, gliding along the bank of the creek, looking in the water. We laughed at her, but later, when we heard the story about the ghostly mother looking for her son, we wondered if Roberta had actually had a glimpse into the past.

The staff goes home after the restaurant closes, so we made sure we heard their stories about ghosts and strange happenings, which I related earlier, before they left. After dinner, the owners gave us our room assignments, and we all settled in. Sharon took Room 5 and Robert took Room 10, both on the second floor. Roberta and I took Room 12 on the third floor.

The staff had gone by then, so Sharon and I decided to get some ice for our rooms from the kitchen. As we started to leave the kitchen with our ice, we heard an extremely loud bang behind us. Startled, we quickly turned around to see what had fallen, but nothing was out of place. All the skillets, pots, and pans were on the shelves where they should be. We took the ice and hurried to our rooms.

Sharon and Robert joined Roberta and me in our room to talk about the stories we had just heard. I pulled up a rocking chair and sat down. I didn't realize that this was the haunted rocking chair where the older man had been seen. Suddenly, something started trying to push me out of the chair! It was the strangest feeling. It happened three times. I guess I had a funny look on my face because the others were staring at me.

"What's wrong, Lonnie?" Sharon asked.

"Something is pushing me!" I said.

"No wonder," Roberta said. "You're probably sitting on the ghost!"

Since all the other chairs were occupied by then, I had to remain in that rocking chair. The ghost must have understood I had nowhere else to sit, because the pushing stopped.

Robert decided to go downstairs to the kitchen to get some ice for his room, too, while Sharon, Roberta, and I remained in Room 12. We were the only guests at the inn at the time, so we left our door unlocked. We knew Robert was coming back to join us. After a few minutes, we all three heard footsteps coming down the hall. We assumed it was Robert returning to our room, but the footsteps stopped at the door. I opened the door, and we all saw that the hall was empty. The footsteps had been loud and distinct, but nobody was there and there was nowhere in the hall for anyone to hide.

A while later, Robert came back to our room. He had been downstairs all this time talking to the owners while we heard the footsteps, so it couldn't have been Robert who was walking down our hall.

After we went to bed, strange noises kept waking up Roberta and me. We thought they were coming from the heating unit and tried to ignore them. Around 3:00 A.M., Roberta and I heard three knocks at our door. When we went to the door, nobody was there. After that, we slept through the night without incident.

The next morning, we all ate a hearty breakfast, took some pictures, and left with some ghostly tales to tell.

Balls of Light

RB: In the dark winter months, balls of light often show up in the strange stories we are told. They have long been a source of mystery. They do not show up in pictures, but they are balls of light that can be seen with the naked eye. Our friend Sharon Brown says she became interested in the paranormal because of an experience with a strange ball of light that appeared in her room.

Sharon was in bed in her room at her family's house in the country in south central Kentucky when it happened. She remembers distinctly that she was not asleep. There in the country at night it was totally dark, with no streetlights to shine through the windows. There were no cars going by, either. But Sharon became aware of a ball of pure white light in her room. She lay very still, for instinctively she knew that movement would scare it away. She watched it for two or three minutes while it went around the room and up and down the walls. Then she turned and it disappeared.

Sharon could never figure out what it was. There was a family cemetery down the road, so she thought maybe it could have come from there.

During the last night my mother was home before she died, I was sitting up with her because she was so ill. I asked the angels to help Mom, and immediately a small ball of pure golden light appeared on the wall and danced across the top of the frame of Mom's favorite picture. After that, she rested easier than she had all day. The next morning, we took her to the hospital, where she died soon after. Was the light an answer from the angels? It couldn't have come from anywhere outside.

My dad, Tom, and his best friend, Edgar, got help one night from a ball of light. It was early winter, and after several rainy days the two young men were bored and looking for something to do.

One of their favorite things to do was to tease a neighbor of theirs named Eli. Eli had shocks of fodder in his cornfield to feed his cattle. He was always concerned that his cows would get in the cornfield and eat too much. Dad and Edgar would wait until dark, sneak into Eli's barn, and take two bells off the cows. Each armed with a bell, they would separate and go to different parts of the cornfield. Eli went to bed early, so they would give him time to get into bed, and then one would ring a cowbell. Eli would jump up, put his clothes on, and come search for his cows. When he couldn't find them, the other prankster would ring his cowbell in another part of the field, and poor Eli would go off hunting in that direction. Dad and Edgar thought this was funny, but it was hard on Eli as he ran back and forth trying to find his cows. Eli never caught on, and the two young men would slip back to the barn and put the bells back on the cows before they returned home.

After it had rained for several days, Dad and Edgar felt the need to get out and get into mischief, so they headed to Eli's house to play their usual trick. They crossed the foot log and noticed that the creek was rising from all the rain they'd had. They reached Eli's house and waited in the barn for his light to go out. They waited and waited, but the light stayed on. They got impatient wondering why he was still up, so they decided to go ahead and ring the bells anyway.

As they started to remove the bells, the dark sky was suddenly lit up by a great ball of fire. Dad and Edgar watched the ball move over Eli's house and rain down fire. They rushed from the barn, thinking the house would catch fire, but nothing ignited.

"Let's get out of here!" said Edgar, and Dad was right behind him.

"Did you ever see anything like that?" Dad asked.

"No!" said Edgar. "What do you suppose it was?"

"I don't know," Dad said. "Maybe it was some kind of warning."

The two walked in silence until they came to the creek. The water was up—now it was touching the bottom of the foot log. Only a sliver of moon lit the sky, and they had not brought a light. The way across the foot log was not clear. One misstep would send them tumbling into the icy water below.

"Do you think we dare cross it?" asked Edgar.

"We have to," Dad said. "It's the only way home unless we walk miles to the road and the bridge."

"Maybe we should do that," suggested Edgar.

While they were trying to decide, a yellow ball of light appeared at the end of the foot log and began moving slowly across it.

"Look at that!" said Dad. "What is it?"

"I don't know," said Edgar, "but look how it's lighting up the foot log! Let's follow it."

"What if it goes out while we are on the log?" asked Dad.

"I've got a feeling it won't," said Edgar. "Come on!"

The two followed the ball of light as it guided them safely across the foot log. Then it simply vanished. The boys were speechless the rest of the way home.

The next day, they learned that Eli's wife was very ill. The doctor had ordered her to rest. If Dad and Edgar had played their game with the cowbells the night before, it would have made Eli's wife even more distressed.

Dad and Edgar decided that the ball of fire over the house was a warning that Eli's wife was ill and the light on the foot log was a reward because they didn't disturb her. But neither one ever figured out where the lights came from.

Mindy's Miracle

RB: Many mysteries in life will never be solved. Sometimes logic simply does not apply. I have heard many stories like the one that follows. I like this version because it's about a college student and I heard it when I was a college student. I identified with Mindy because graduating meant so much to me.

With the sound of "Pomp and Circumstance" playing in her head, Mindy stood looking at the cap and gown hanging in the closet and waited for the sound of footsteps in the hall. She knew her dad would come tonight, for tonight wouldn't be a rehearsal. Tonight, after a struggle too long and painful to think about, Mindy would be graduating from college.

Mindy wished she could have graduated in June, when the graduation ceremony was more of an event, but she was graduating after midterm in January. She had reduced her class load to take a job while she was in school, so it had taken her four and a half years to finish. She could have taken additional classes and waited till the following June to graduate, but she had a job offer that she needed to take. It was time to move on.

Mindy's dad had helped her all he could, but his wages as a coal miner certainly didn't make him rich. Together, though, they had managed. Since Mindy's mom died, her dad had seemed to live for this night to see his daughter graduate. It was almost time now for the ceremony to start. He would surely be here soon.

Mindy flipped on the radio, but turned it off again. She had no time for such a minor diversion. She finished getting dressed in silence.

The dorm was full of hustle and bustle. Mindy heard a voice call from down the hall, "Hurry! It's almost time to go!"

Mindy was already on her way out. She had to meet the last bus at the campus bus station.

Mindy watched anxiously as the passengers stepped off the bus one by one, but her dad was not among them. She couldn't understand it. Her dad had never broken a promise to her before. She had almost given up, but looked around one more time to make sure she hadn't missed him. When she turned back, she saw her father come rushing up. As she ran toward him, she saw that something was wrong. Her father's head was bandaged.

"What happened, Dad? Are you all right?" she asked.

"Just a little accident," he said. "I guess my head got in the way of some falling rock in the mine today. Now, come on. I'll walk with you. You don't want to be late for the ceremony."

The dorm was near the auditorium.

"I've got to run in and get my cap and gown," Mindy said. "I'll be right back. Wait here for me."

"Here," her dad said quickly, taking a small package from his coat pocket. "Take this with you. I couldn't get you anything for your graduation, but I do have something for you. It's your mother's Bible. It's from both of us. When you read it, think of all the dreams we've had for you. Don't ever stop believing, no matter what. Miracles do happen, Mindy!"

"Thank you, Dad," she said, hugging him as she took the package.

"Hurry, now!" he told her.

"You're cold," said Mindy. "Do you want to come in with me?"

"No, I'm fine," he assured her. "The ceremony's about to start. I'll meet you over there."

Mindy rushed to the dorm, set down her father's package on her desk, put on her cap and gown, and raced to the auditorium. Soon she was one of the students marching proudly across the stage to receive a diploma. As it was placed in her hand, she glanced over at the softly lighted doorway and saw her dad standing there, smiling.

As soon as the ceremony was over, Mindy ran to look for her dad. Faces swirled around her, but she was looking for only one. Then a hand touched her arm and she whirled around, expecting to see her father. Instead, she was looking at the grim face of the dean of women.

"I need to talk to you, Mindy," she said.

"Sure," said Mindy, "but I'm looking for my dad right now."

"This is about your dad," said the dean.

Mindy remembered the bandage and thought he must have passed out.

"Where is he?" she asked. "Is he okay?"

"We got a call from the mine," the dean said. "There was an accident today. There was a cave-in just as your dad's shift ended this afternoon. He was killed instantly. I'm so sorry, Mindy."

"No," said Mindy. "That's impossible!"

"It was announced on the radio before the graduation ceremony started, but one of the girls said your radio was off. I decided not to tell you until now because I thought he would want it this way. I know how much this night meant to both of you."

"He's not dead," said Mindy. "He can't be!"

"Is there anything I can do?" asked the dean.

Mindy stood there stunned, but she managed to stammer, "N-no, thank you. I would like to be alone for a while."

Mindy walked slowly back to the dorm. The pieces were beginning to fit now. Her father's head was bandaged. He was cold. He was dead. But how could that be? Had she imagined the whole thing?

Snowflakes began to fall, and silent tears fell on Mindy's cheeks. The crisp new diploma in her hand reminded her that tonight hadn't been a dream.

She entered the dormitory and felt sympathetic eyes on

her as she walked down the hall. She would not tell them what happened, for nobody would believe in such a miracle.

Mindy closed the door to her room behind her and clicked on the light. She unwrapped the small package on her desk and sat down on her bed. Then nothing broke the silence but the rustle of the pages as she read her mother's Bible.

When the Crows Fly

RB: Even though I have not figured out the answers to many strange things I've experienced, I am glad my life has been filled with mystery and wonder. Some things that I once considered to be only superstitions turned out to be warnings.

There are many superstitions about crows, as I learned from my Irish heritage. Those black feathers conjure up all sorts of ideas. To see one crow is a bad omen. To see two crows means good luck. Three mean health, and four mean wealth. Five crows mean sickness. To see six or more crows means death. We were used to sayings like that when I was growing up, and we didn't take them seriously. Then something happened that made me wonder.

In 2007, I was hired to do a three-day writing workshop from January 30 through February 1 in Corbin, Kentucky, at St. Camillus Montessori School. I was to work with a wide age range of students, from three-year-olds to eighth graders. In this workshop I would be working with some age groups I'd not worked with before, so I set about making lesson plans and writing new material.

This was a very difficult time for my family and me. My sister Fatima, who had been bedridden at home for three years from a stroke, had to be transferred to a nursing home, much against her wishes. It had become impossible for us to continue to care properly for her at home, so she had to accept the inevitable. We were all upset about it, but eventually Fatima was moved to a nursing home in Mt. Juliet, Tennessee, on January 15, 2007.

A couple of weeks into her stay, she seemed to be adjusting well, but I couldn't get her off my mind. The thought kept popping into my mind that I should go see her. But even though the feeling was urgent, I really needed to continue with my workshop preparations.

"We'll go see her February 2, just as soon as we get back," I told Lonnie.

Lonnie said, "Let's go now. You'll feel better when you see that she's all right. You'll do fine with the workshops."

"You're right," I agreed. "Let's go."

I put aside my work, and we drove down for a two-day visit. Fatima was in better spirits than I expected her to be. Her roommate's sister was there visiting, too, so we all told stories and laughed until people were sticking their heads in the door to see what was going on. The second day, we took Lonnie's manuscript (*Stories You Won't Believe*), which was in the process of being published, to Fatima's room. We read over all the stories and reminisced about the good old days when we were growing up together.

I was in a better state of mind when Lonnie and I left for

Corbin. The workshops went well. The staff, students, and parents at St. Camillus were absolutely wonderful and helpful. Lonnie and I stayed at a motel near the school so it would be easy to get back and forth.

The first night at the motel, we looked out the window and were amazed to see the sky full of crows! Hundreds and hundreds of them circled the motel and never came down. I thought of an old Irish legend that referred to such an incident as a warning of a coming death, but I tried to put it out of my mind. We asked several people about the crows, but they had never seen anything like it either.

The second night, the crows again filled the sky over the motel, flying around and around in circles. Lonnie and I had both grown up in the country, but we had never seen crows fly at night like that. It reminded us of Alfred Hitchcock's classic movie *The Birds*.

The third night, the crows returned, filling the night sky once again as they circled above us. It gave me an eerie, but sad, feeling.

"I think it's a warning," I told Lonnie, hoping even as I said it that it wasn't true. "I think Fatima is going to die."

On February 1, my last day at St. Camillus, the forecast was calling for snow. I hoped it would hold off until we could get back to Louisville.

As we drove to school that morning, we passed the old residence hall where the sisters used to live. They had told us at dinner the night before that the building was condemned, closed, and locked. When I asked about ghosts possibly being there, the nuns revealed that they did have some reports about someone being seen inside at the window on the top floor. I wasn't looking at the window as we approached that morning, but I suddenly heard a loud "Caw!"

I looked up and saw one single crow. I remembered that seeing one crow was a bad sign.

As it flew off, I looked at the window. The curtain was pulled back, and a woman was staring down at us. The image wasn't menacing or comforting, but the face looked sad. In an instant, it was gone. Was it trying to tell me something? Or was it just a spooky old house playing tricks? It was gone so fast, I wasn't even sure I'd seen it.

I finished the workshop that day without further incident. Lonnie and I headed home with the snow coming right behind us. We made it home just as the snow and ice hit. I had barely put my purse down when the phone rang. The caller told me that Fatima had died a few minutes earlier in the nursing home. It was February 1. If we had waited until February 2 to go see her, it would have been too late. Maybe the crows flew those three nights around the motel to warn me of the news I would get when I got home.

Fatima's Visits

RB: Before my sister Fatima died, she and I made a pact that whoever went first would come back and visit the other. She would add with a laugh that, first, she would visit with all the friends and relatives on the other side that she hadn't seen for a long time. Next, she would fly to Hawaii and New Orleans (two places she'd never been). Only after that would she come see me. I joked back that I would count on seeing her then a few weeks after she died.

February 4, 2007, the day of Fatima's funeral, was snowy and bitter cold. The graveside service was short, but standing there for even that brief time chilled me. I became very ill with an upper respiratory infection, which lasted for about three months. During that time I was too miserable to think of my sister's promise to visit.

The medication I was taking left my mouth dry, so I often got up for water throughout the night. One night about nine weeks after Fatima died, I woke up a little after 2:00 A.M. and started down the hall to the kitchen to get a drink. I suddenly became aware of a warm glow coming from the side of my kitchen that was out of my view. There was nothing on that side of the kitchen to make that glow, but I felt a strong presence there. I knew it wasn't a human intruder, but *something* was in there waiting for me. I simply did not have the strength to confront whatever was there. I was so ill and shaky that I couldn't make myself take another step in that direction. I gulped a drink in the bathroom and made my way back to bed. I lay in bed wondering if it could have been my sister.

I fell asleep immediately and dreamed very vividly of Fatima. She was dressed in bright purple pants with a matching flowered top. It was the kind of outfit she always liked to wear. The miraculous thing was that she was walking.

"Sis!" I said. "It's great to see you walk again!"

"Yes," she answered. "I'm a little shaky, but I'm getting there!"

She went on to tell me that she was fine. She was going places and visiting people. My dream ended as Fatima was walking up a hill in the sunshine. Children and pets were all around her, and she stopped to talk to the children and pet the animals, just as she would have done in life.

When I woke up, I felt very comforted. Even if I had missed a chance to see Fatima in my kitchen, I had at least had a nice visit with her in my dream.

I believe I received one more communication from Fatima. This one came through a friend, Rick Hayes, a gifted, sensitive man who seems to have a unique talent of communicating with the dead. (I must admit that I am somewhat skeptical when someone tells me he can do this, but I try to keep an open mind.)

Rick is an inspirational speaker, so when he came to Louisville the fall after Fatima's death, a friend and I went to hear him. After Rick finished speaking, he allowed a period of time for questions and answers from the audience. Some asked him questions about their loved ones.

"Ask him about your sister," my friend urged.

"No," I said. "If I am supposed to get a message, I will."

While Rick was on the other side of the room giving messages to others, I sat with my hands in my lap, thinking *Sister, sister, sister.*

Suddenly Rick turned, walked across the room, and

stopped in front of me. He put his hands to his temples and said aloud, "Sister, sister, sister. Somebody here wants to know about her sister. And it's you!" He looked straight at me.

He then told me, "She's happy. She's with friends and family, and she thanks you for the care you gave her when she was alive. She says she came to visit you about nine weeks after she died. So you'll know it was her, she says to tell you that she was in the room where she would least likely be—the kitchen."

That was very impressive to me. Rick could not have known that Fatima hated kitchens. She always said that her dream house would be a house without a kitchen. That information could only have come from my sister Fatima.

A Christmas Gift from Fatima

RB: Fatima was ten years older than I, but we were always very close. She loved holidays, especially Christmas, and always tried to get everybody an unusual Christmas gift. Even after she had a stroke, she would send us shopping for unusual things she thought of for family and friends.

She once insisted that my nephew's girlfriend, Fran, buy me a rooster cookie jar that she'd seen in an ad. Fran bought it, but she reminded Fatima that I had no great love for roosters, because Mom had owned a couple of roosters that would fight me when I was a child. I'd run to Fatima and say with my childish lisp, "Thister! Thister! The old rooster's after me!" She would always come to my aid. Through the years, that had become a joke between us. When one of us would have a problem of any kind, we'd call the other and say, "Thister! Thister! The old rooster's after me!" And the other would help solve the problem.

As I opened Fatima's gift that Christmas morning, Fran said, "I want you to know that I did not pick that for you. Fatima did. You won't like it!"

Fatima sat there laughing until I saw the rooster cookie jar. Fran was surprised when I burst out laughing, too. We shared our joke with her about the rooster.

Immediately after she'd had her stroke, Fatima seemed to improve, but after some falls and more mini-strokes, she ended up bedridden. I helped her all I could for three long years, but her condition eventually got to the point where none of us could care properly for her at home. She had to be placed in a nursing home, where she'd hoped and prayed she'd never be. The old rooster had indeed reared its ugly head, and I had failed to help her. I felt very burdened by that failure when Fatima died on February 1, 2007.

Christmas of 2007 was the first Christmas in my entire life that I had spent apart from my older sister. Regardless of where we were, we always managed to get together for Christmas. I really missed Fatima through the holiday, and I half expected her to appear in some ghostly form. That didn't happen, however. I felt like she was near me, but I saw no sign.

Late Christmas night, I was sitting in the living room

alone, thinking about all the good times my sister and I had had at Christmases in the past, when an amazing thing happened.

One Christmas when I was in the second grade, Fatima helped me memorize a long poem, "Two Little Stockings," for a Christmas program at school. It wasn't a great poem, but we enjoyed it. Through the years, we had tried to find a copy, but neither of us could remember the author or the name of the book it was in. We could only remember the title and the first four lines. I had typed this information into my computer several times and tried searching the Internet, but I couldn't find it. I would get ads about ladies' stockings, but never a poem.

On this night, Fatima's face flashed vividly in my mind. I knew she was near me. She was radiant and laughing as she sent me a mental message: *Go to the computer and look for the poem!* Part of me resisted as her face faded. I felt it would be just another useless search, but the urge to look for that poem was irresistible. I went to the computer, typed in the title and the first four lines, and up came the entire poem! I couldn't believe it. I printed a copy immediately.

Someone with a blog for home schooling had just posted it. He had written that he didn't even know why he had posted that particular poem because he didn't think it was an especially great poem. He said it came from an anthology published in the early 1900s for second graders to memorize. He felt it was too difficult for second graders, but he wrote, "Here it is for whatever it's worth."

Fatima's face came back to my mind as I held a copy of the poem. She gave me another mental message: *Stop worrying. It's okay. Think about the good things and move on.*

The worry about her and the burden I felt immediately lifted. I knew she understood that her condition after the stroke was one old rooster too big for me to defeat. Realizing this was a great gift.

Then I realized she had given me an unusual gift that was tangible, too. I was holding the poem I would never have looked for if it hadn't been for her urging me mentally to go to the computer.

There is an amusing postscript to this story. Through the years that I taught at Southern Middle School, my friend Pat, the school secretary, and I always exchanged stories that were odd or coincidental. After my experience that night with Fatima's messages, I immediately e-mailed Pat, telling her what had happened with the poem. On the subject line of my message I wrote "Weird Story." Pat called me later to tell me that she had received my e-mail and had read it.

"I tried to reply," she told me, "but the oddest thing happened. On my subject line, it flashed, 'Weird Story has changed! Weird Story has changed!' Then the message vanished! I couldn't find it under save, delete, or old mail. I think your sister is messing with my computer!"

Pat and I got a laugh out of this, and I think Fatima did, too. It all could be a coincidence, but I prefer to think that Fatima will always find a way to stay in touch.

Love Lives On

RB: I saved this story for last because of the message it sends. It is hard for me to write it because these are my friends and I know how deeply they feel their loss.

I taught with Annie in middle school for several years. When we retired, we kept in touch. Christmas was a special time for us to catch up on everything that had happened during the year. We didn't write a Christmas form letter; we sent a personal, handwritten letter updating each other about our activities. I could hardly wait to open the envelope when I saw her name on it because she and her husband, Jim, had such fun adventures. Annie's stepdaughter, Susan, brought her great joy, and this came through whenever Annie spoke of her. And I could always count on a funny story about her cats.

This year, I wrote Annie early and told her that Lonnie and I were working on a book of true ghost stories.

"Do you have any ghost stories to tell me?" I wrote.

I got a call from Annie.

"Roberta, Jim died last winter," she said. "Some strange things have been happening, and I'd be glad to share them with you."

I was stunned. I held the phone and listened to her words, but they didn't want to register in my mind. Jim had begun having pain in his chest. The doctors had checked it, thinking it was his heart. They learned it was his lungs instead. There were complications, and the doctors hadn't been able to save him. It was unbelievable, but Jim was gone. Since he had died, though, things had been happening to Annie and Susan that made them believe he was still near them.

I met Annie and Susan for lunch to hear the details.

"I held Jim as he died," Annie told me. "He was heavily sedated. As I talked to him, two tiny orbs of blue moving light appeared in front of his beautiful blue irises. Even in this horrific time, I was stunned by the beauty and wonder of the orbs. They were my gift from Jim—a calming distraction from what was happening to him. Then, just moments before the nurse informed me that he was gone, the orbs faded. Of course, I already knew."

"As Dad was dying," said Susan, "I was thinking, *Dad give me a sign through the TV so I'll know you're all right*. He was really into watching TV, so I thought he might use it to signal. Nothing happened at the hospital, though.

"Dad and Annie had given my husband and me a TV that didn't work, but Dad was going to get it fixed for us. After he died, I went home from the hospital feeling very sad. Suddenly the broken TV came on and started changing channels. The VCR and the DVD players went on and off, too. That had never happened before! Was Dad trying to signal me?

"I decided to take a shower to calm myself down. When I came out of the shower, the lights and the fan in the room started going on and off. It was kind of scary. No other part of the house was affected.

"My husband didn't really believe me when I told him what had happened. He thought I was just being emotional over Dad's death. Then, in his presence, the broken TV came on again and did all the things it had done when I was watching alone. I said, 'Okay, Dad, we'll get the TV fixed.' Right then, it stopped!

"Later, when I was driving, the car doors would unlock as soon as I locked them. The dome light would come on and wouldn't go off. I said, 'Dad, I can't drive with the light on. Please stop.' The light went off and the doors stayed locked.

"Another time, when I was writing an e-mail at work, I noticed something inserted in it. It said, 'I spoke easily.' Was it Dad? I know I didn't write it."

"Have you felt him near after he died?" I asked Annie.

"Once when I was going down the basement steps," Annie replied, "I think he pushed me gently. He was always telling me to be careful on the steps. This time I was on the third step from the bottom when I felt something give me a little push. I heard his voice in my head: *I am not here to remind you now, so remember to be careful.*

"Another time after I'd had a little get-together for his friends, I felt his hand on my shoulder. He gave it a little squeeze as if to say thanks. Every day, I feel his love. I always will."

I reminded Annie that I usually heard a cat story from her and that I missed that.

"Oh, I have one of those, too," she told me. "We had two cats, Pooh and Pounce. Pooh was sixteen years old and

Pounce was twenty. Pooh learned how to open our cabinet doors and would rattle pots and pans in the cabinet. We had to have Pooh put down, and soon after that we would hear the cabinet door open, followed by all the noises Pooh had made when he was alive. This went on until Pounce died a while later. Then we never heard the sounds any more. We figured Pooh was just waiting around for Pounce to join her."

If you are still a skeptic, we hope you still were able to enjoy the stories we have told here. If you are a believer, as we are, then you will be happy in thinking our loved ones are waiting on the other side for us to join them—just like Pooh waited for Pounce. It is comforting to think that love lasts forever and life goes on after death, just like the ghosts here in Kentucky—season after season.

SUGGESTED READING

Brown, Alan. *Haunted Kentucky: Ghosts and Strange Phenomena of the Bluegrass State.* Mechanicsburg, Pa.: Stackpole Books, 2009.

Brown, Lonnie E. *Stories You Won't Believe.* Baltimore: PublishAmerica, 2007.

Brown, Roberta Simpson. *The Walking Trees and Other Scary Stories.* Little Rock: August House, 1991.

Dominé, David. *Ghosts of Old Louisville.* Kuttawa, Ky.: McClanahan Publishing House, 2005.

——. *Haunts of Old Louisville.* Kuttawa, Ky.: McClanahan Publishing House, 2009.

——. *Phantoms of Old Louisville.* Kuttawa, Ky.: McClanahan Publishing House, 2006.

Freese, Thomas. *Shaker Ghost Stories from Pleasant Hill, Kentucky.* Bloomington, Ind.: AuthorHouse, 2005.

——. *Ghosts, Spirits, and Angels: True Tales from Kentucky and Beyond.* Morley, Mo.: Acclaim Press, 2009.

Gibson, Willie "Windwalker." *The Shaman Windwalker.* Bloomington, Ind.: AuthorHouse, 2002.

——. *Soul Warriors.* Baltimore: PublishAmerica, 2009.

Hargrove, Wanda D. *Ghostly Tales of Kentucky.* Baltimore: PublishAmerica, 2006.

———. *Waiting for the Shadows.* Baltimore: PublishAmerica, 2007.

Johnson, Larry. *The Seelbach.* Louisville, Ky.: Butler Books, 2005.

McCormick, James, and Macy Wyatt. *Ghosts of the Bluegrass.* Lexington: University Press of Kentucky, 2009.

Montell, W. Lynwood. *Ghosts across Kentucky.* Lexington: University Press of Kentucky, 2000.

———. *Ghosts along the Cumberland.* Knoxville: University of Tennessee Press, 1975.

———. *Haunted Houses and Family Ghosts of Kentucky.* Lexington: University Press of Kentucky, 2001.

———. *Kentucky Ghosts.* Lexington: University Press of Kentucky, 1994.

Olson, Colleen O'Connor, and Charles Hanion. *Scary Stories of Mammoth Cave.* St. Louis: Cave Books, 2002.

Parker, Robert W. *Haunted Louisville.* Decatur, Ill.: Whitechapel Press, 2007.

———. *Haunted Louisville—beyond Downtown.* Decatur, Ill.: Whitechapel Press, 2010.

Taylor, Troy. *Down in the Darkness.* Alton, Ill.: Whitechapel Press, 2003.

Taylor, Troy, and Len Adams. *So There I Was.* Decatur, Ill.: Whitechapel Press, 2006.

GHOSTLY PLACES
TO VISIT

Shaker Village is located on U.S. Highway 68, twenty-five miles southeast of Lexington and seven miles northeast of Harrodsburg, Kentucky. It is accessible from I-75 and I-64. The address is 3501 Lexington Road, Harrodsburg, Kentucky, 40330. Call 1-800-734-5611 or visit their Web site at www .shakervillageky.org for more information.

For those who would like to visit **Berea,** campus tours are available. You can visit craft shops, student industries, the Boone Tavern Hotel, the college store, and many places on campus that reflect an accurate picture of Appalachian life. For more information, call 859-985-3005 or check the Web site at www.berea.edu.

If you would like to tour the *Belle of Louisville* and see what you may experience there, it is docked at Fourth and River Road in downtown Louisville, Kentucky. Call for information about schedules and ticket prices at the summer office (502-582-2547) or the winter office (502-778-6651). Remember, officially you will not encounter any ghosts, but unofficially, you never know what will happen!

If you want to go to the **Palace Theater** to see a show, you might encounter a ghostly presence yourself. The address is 625 South Fourth Street in downtown Louisville.

If you are interested in booking a tour of **Waverly,** call 502-933-2142 Monday through Friday between 9:00 A.M. and 5:00 P.M. You can learn more by logging on to the Web site: www .therealwaverlyhills.com.

We highly recommend **The Poet's House** to anyone who wants an unforgettable getaway. The hosts are gracious, the food is great, and the view of the Ohio River, with the hills of Indiana as a backdrop, is breathtaking. It is located at 501 Main Street in Ghent, Kentucky, about halfway between Louisville and Cincinnati off Interstate 71. For reservations or for more information about the house, contact the proprietors, David Hendren and Rick Whitfill, at 502-347-0135 or at poetshouse@bellsouth.net.

If you would like to experience the mystery of **Magnolia House** yourself, we highly recommend that you go for a visit. This is one of the nicest, friendliest places we have ever stayed. Magnolia House is located at the corner of James and

Merchant Streets in Columbia, Kentucky. Call Carson or Linda Lewis at 270-378-6243 or 270-634-0694 or e-mail cllewis@duocounty.com for more information or reservations. You can also check out their Web site for more information and pictures at www.bedandbreakfastmagnoliahouse.com. The room that had the mysterious moving rug is the Serenity Room on the first floor, pictured on the Web site.

Anyone interested in visiting **Doe Run Inn** can log on to the Web site at www.doeruninn.com or call 270-422-2982. The inn is located at 500 Doe Run Hotel Road in Brandenburg, Kentucky, 40108, just forty-four miles outside of Louisville going toward Fort Knox.

About the Authors

Roberta Simpson Brown and **Lonnie E. Brown** were born in Russell Springs, Kentucky, near Lake Cumberland; they now live in Louisville. Their families were friends for generations, so Lonnie and Roberta share a common background of storytelling that flourished in rural south central Kentucky. Married since 1977, they enjoy reading, traveling, and learning about the paranormal. Lonnie is an accomplished golfer and musician. Roberta is a retired teacher who now works as a professional storyteller. Roberta and Lonnie coauthored *Spooky, Kooky Poems for Kids*. Lonnie is the author of *Stories You Won't Believe*. Roberta is the author of *The Walking Trees and Other Scary Stories*, *Queen of the Cold-Blooded Tales*, *Scared in School*, *Lamplight Tales*, and the coauthor of *Strains of Music* with her sister, the late Fatima Atchley.